"I want you to come with me," Tracker said

He took Sophie's hand, leading her away from the rest of the party guests. His gaze never left hers as he slipped a card out of his pocket and gave it to her.

She glanced down at the card, recognizing it as the "quickie on demand" coupon she'd given him earlier. "Here?" she croaked.

"And now. Those are the rules of the game as you explained them to me, right?"

"Tracker, I—"

"Are you having second thoughts about our deal?" he asked as he led her down a hallway and opened the first door. It was a powder room, with barely enough room for one person between the toilet and the sink. He led her inside, and suddenly the term "close quarters" took on a whole new meaning.

"I'm collecting on that coupon, princess. Unless you want to back out?"

Sophie's chin shot up. "I don't back out of agreements."

Tracker nodded, stepping back against the door. "Then I think you should take off your panties...."

Dear Reader,

Sophie Wainwright and Tracker McBride fascinated me from the moment they appeared on the pages of my first Blaze novel—*Intent To Seduce*. The rich "Princess" and the "Shadow" who had the challenging job of protecting her struck sparks off each other even when they were separated by a continent. So how could I not write their story?

The last person in the world that Sophie wants to be attracted to is Tracker McBride. As chief of security for her brother's business, he's made it clear that he thinks of her only as a job. For one whole year he's kept his professional distance, watching over her from afar. Sophie's problem? She hasn't forgotten what it felt like to have Tracker's hands on her—even briefly. How *can* she forget when he touches her more and more intimately each night in her dreams? She can't even date other men without *seeing* Tracker, *feeling* Tracker. Sophie's solution? If she's ever going to get her love life back to normal she has to get Tracker McBride out of her dreams and into her bed *for real*. And to do that, she'll play any sensual game it takes!

I hope you enjoy watching these two very reluctant people play the riskiest game of all. Let me know. You can write to me at P.O. Box 718, Fayetteville, NY 13066, or visit my Web site—www.carasummers.com.

Enjoy,

Cara Summers

Books by Cara Summers

GAME FOR ANYTHING

Cara Summers

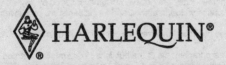

HARLEQUIN®

TORONTO • NEW YORK • LONDON
AMSTERDAM • PARIS • SYDNEY • HAMBURG
STOCKHOLM • ATHENS • TOKYO • MILAN • MADRID
PRAGUE • WARSAW • BUDAPEST • AUCKLAND

To my editor Brenda Chin—writing coach, book doctor
and muse. Thanks for always being able to see what
I'm trying to do—and then making me go back and do it!

ISBN 0-373-79075-9

GAME FOR ANYTHING

Copyright © 2003 by Carolyn Hanlon.

This edition published by arrangement with Harlequin Books S.A.

® and TM are trademarks of the publisher. Trademarks indicated with
® are registered in the United States Patent and Trademark Office, the
Canadian Trade Marks Office and in other countries.

Visit us at www.eHarlequin.com

Printed in U.S.A.

Prologue

"YOU'RE SAFE NOW, Princess."

Sophie's fear streamed away the moment she heard him. He would set her free.

The cloth covering her eyes and mouth prevented her from seeing him, from saying his name, but she recognized his voice, his touch. Just the barest brush of his fingers along her throat made her skin burn and her blood heat.

In the three days since her kidnapping, she'd known that Tracker McBride would come for her. She'd steeled herself against his anger for tricking him and making him chase her across the country. But his hands were gentle, his voice soothing.

"Don't be afraid."

He would touch her now—to make sure she was all right. The anticipation of it made her tremble. The reality of it, the press of those long, lean fingers as they moved over her shoulders and down the length of her arms, left every inch of her skin quivering and then burning.

Her response was always like this—basic, primitive. He touched and she wanted. Desire twisted into a hard knot, and her body began to move, lifting, aching to get closer.

When he gripped her waist, heat, a searing flame, streamed through her. Muscles deep inside of her clenched and her hips arched upward. *More.* But his hands moved on, continuing their slow, thorough journey over her hips and down her legs. Torturing her.

"I'll have you free in a minute," he said as he removed the blindfold and the gag. "Don't open your eyes right away."

The moment her arms were untied, she wrapped them around him and held him tight. *Safe.* Now he would free her from the terrible heat he'd built inside of her. He had to. He stroked one hand down her hair, then she felt his fingers slip beneath her chin and lift it.

"Please…" She wasn't even sure it was her voice that had said the word. But his mouth brushed against hers and his tongue moistened her lips.

"Now." With a will of its own, her body melted, molding itself to every hard plane and angle of his. It wasn't enough. She wanted him right where that deep, demanding ache tugged at her very center. Threading her fingers through his hair, she arched against him. *Soon…please.*

Finally, when she thought she might die of the wanting, his mouth grew harder, more insistent, and his hand moved to the inside of her thigh.

Yes. Almost. Need built razor sharp as she arched against him, urging him on. The tension inside of her built, twisted, tightened. When his fingers finally slipped into her, the climax moved through her at once, building higher and higher until, deep inside of her, pleasure exploded.

It was the sound of her own voice crying out that shot Sophie out of the dream. For a moment, she lay there, shuddering in the aftermath of the release that had nearly shattered her. She was gripping the bed-clothes in her fists, sweat was cooling on her skin and her breath was coming in short pants. Opening her eyes, she saw that Chess, her cat, was peering down at her.

"I'm fine," she murmured, releasing a fistful of sheet so that she could run her hand over her large, plump guardian angel.

The cat snorted in disbelief.

Sophie sighed. Chess had been a gift from her brother, Lucas, when she'd moved out of the family home into her living quarters over One of a Kind, the antique and specialty store she ran in Georgetown. They'd been together for five years now, and Chess's main joy in life seemed to stem from making her be honest with herself.

"All right. All right." Sitting up, Sophie ran a hand through her hair. "I'm not fine." How could she be when the best sex—the only sex—she'd had in over a year was occurring only in her dreams?

And the dream was being triggered by a man who annoyed the hell out of her in real life. Tracker McBride, or as she called him, "The Shadow." Two years ago her brother had hired him to head up the security at Wainwright Enterprises, but as far as Sophie could tell, Tracker's mission statement read: "Keep the spoiled, misfit sister from destroying Wainwright Enterprises."

The inescapable fact that she'd come close to doing

that twice now—by hooking up with fortune hunters who were after the Wainwright money—humiliated and infuriated her. Having her weakness and stupidity exposed by a complete stranger had only added salt to the wound. Tracker McBride now knew what everyone else in the family knew: she just wasn't good enough to be a Wainwright.

Tracker's continued surveillance of her during the past year only confirmed that her brother still didn't trust her. Every time she went out at night to meet friends, she could sense Tracker's presence. At times, she was sure that she could feel his gaze moving over her, and the sensation was so intense that he might as well have been touching her. But he never came close enough for her to spot him.

Except in her dreams.

"Damn it." Rising, she scooped Chess up from the bed and headed toward the kitchen "I've got to get free of him."

Chess snorted again.

"No, you don't." Settling the cat on the counter, she pointed an accusing finger at him. "I'm speaking the truth. For the past year, I've been having dreams about this phantom lover who never comes near me in real life. And as long as I have him, I don't want anyone else."

Chess made no comment.

"It's pathetic." Taking a beer out of the refrigerator, she poured it into a saucer and set it in front of him. Then she grabbed her vice of choice—cold pizza.

"I certainly don't want John Landry." There. She'd said it out loud.

Chess rubbed against her arm.

"You think you're a regular truth serum, don't you?"

Chess returned to his beer.

Glancing down at the pizza, Sophie realized she'd lost her appetite. She'd been dating John Landry for two weeks, and he was everything she should want in a man—good-looking, sweet, attentive and rich enough so that Lucas wouldn't have to worry he was after the Wainwright money. He even shared her passion for the antique business.

The problem was, two weeks of dating him had not freed her from her dreams of Tracker. If tonight was any example, dating John had only intensified her desire for The Shadow.

She put the pizza back in the refrigerator untouched.

"I'm going to have to dump John."

Chess's silence indicated his agreement.

"Rejection sucks." She'd experienced enough of it from her parents that she didn't like doing it to anyone. But it wasn't fair to keep dating John Landry. Even now it was difficult for her to conjure up an image of him. The minute she thought she'd captured his blond hair and lean, aristocratic face, the features blurred into the more roughly hewn cheekbones and dark unruly hair of Tracker McBride.

"Damn the man!" She had to stop thinking about him.

The moment Chess lapped up the last drop of beer, she scooped him up and carried him to the couch. "Movie time." With any luck she'd find an old classic on a cable station that would distract her, then lull her into a dreamless sleep.

After two minutes of dedicated channel surfing, she located one of her favorites, *To Catch a Thief.* Settling back against the cushions, she watched Grace Kelly drive a convertible up into the hills of Monte Carlo with Cary Grant at her side. The woman was on a mission. She wanted Cary, and she was going to get him.

Sophie could identify with Grace. She'd always thought of herself as a strong, determined woman, willing to take risks—before she'd taken one too many and gotten herself kidnapped. Thank God, she'd been rescued by Tracker McBride.

Cary Grant was definitely worth wanting. When the movie was made, he'd been at his prime, and the character of the handsome, dangerous jewel thief had suited him to a T. He reminded Sophie a little of Tracker. Both had that air of danger and mystery about them.

All she really knew about The Shadow was that he and Lucas had flown missions together in the service, missions that Lucas would never talk about. Cary Grant's character had secrets, too. And there was one more thing that reminded her of Tracker—the reformed jewel thief in the movie didn't want to have anything to do with the rich, spoiled American that Grace was playing.

Of course, that hadn't slowed Grace down one bit. Plus the whole time she was seducing Grant's character on-screen, she'd been equally busy offscreen, nabbing herself a prince. Sophie was willing to bet that the woman hadn't broken a sweat doing either.

Cool, smart, determined. Sophie had to admire someone like that. Eyes narrowing, she watched Grace Kelly open a picnic basket and laugh teasingly at something Cary said.

Sophie was going to see Tracker at the anniversary party tomorrow. Lucas was recreating every detail of their wedding for his wife, Mac—and Tracker wouldn't dare stay away. He'd been the best man. Sophie's mind raced. She could invite John Landry to go with her—and why not Carter Mitchell, too? He managed the gallery next to her shop, and he wouldn't mind doing her a favor. If she arrived with two men, Tracker might… *No.*

"No, I am not, I repeat, *not* thinking of seducing Tracker McBride."

Chess growled deep in his throat, his disbelief clear.

"Shut up." But the cat was right as usual. She *was* thinking of doing just that. Why should Grace have all the fun? And why should Sophie spend another night just having Tracker in her dreams?

Being a good girl and dating the kind of men that she knew her brother would approve of hadn't worked. Maybe the only way to break free from the trap she found herself in was to seduce the man who held her there….

1

"LUCAS, WILL YOU TAKE this woman to be your lawfully wedded wife?"

Sophie blinked back a tear as her brother said yes. She'd never thought of Lucas as being romantic, but marriage had changed him.

"Mac, will you take Lucas to be your lawfully wedded husband?"

Sophie blinked again as her best friend repeated her vow. As the maid of honor, Sophie stood in attendance behind the bride, elbow to elbow with the best man, Tracker McBride. It was bad enough that every pore in her body seemed to be aware of him—she was not going to cry in front of him!

"By the power invested in me..."

Sophie sniffed as a tear slid down her cheek. The game plan she'd come up with to grab Tracker's attention was not going well. It hadn't mattered one bit that she'd arrived with two men in attendance. The Shadow hadn't appeared until it was time to escort her from the patio outside Lucas's office to the trellis in the rose garden. And all it had taken was the brief, impersonal press of his hand on the small of her back to reawaken her fantasy of having his hands touch every part of her. Just thinking about it had her skin feeling hot and icy at the same time.

Sophie blinked away a second tear. Damn it! Grace Kelly hadn't cried in front of Cary Grant. She'd been all smiles and champagne picnics and dogged determination. More importantly, she'd had a game plan that worked.

"I now pronounce you man and wife."

When Lucas and Mac turned to embrace each other, Sophie felt the second tear slide down her cheek. They shared what she'd always wanted—that closeness with a person you loved and who loved you back.

Hoping that no one would notice, she raised a hand slowly, intending to wipe the tears away. Tracker's arm brushed against hers when he stepped closer and pressed a handkerchief into her hand, and she felt heat streak right down to her toes.

"You okay, Princess?"

Okay? How could she be okay when her insides had become as liquid as the tears running down her face? And when the man who was responsible was treating her like a kid sister? Dabbing at her eyes, she managed a nod.

Wasn't that the story of her life? The men who wanted to seduce her were after her money, and the one man she *wanted* to seduce her was perfectly content to merely watch over her like a protective older brother.

Blinking rapidly, Sophie willed the tears to stop. She'd come here to change that. If plan A—making Tracker jealous—had been a bust, she'd just have to come up with another one. Quick.

As she watched her brother and her best friend turn to face the applause of their guests, she stepped to the side and, for a moment, let her eyes meet Tracker's. When a jolt moved through her right down to her toes, she waited a beat, then two, for her system to stabilize. Dressed all in black, he exuded an air of mystery and danger. And sex—raw, primitive and irresistible.

She was in trouble. It was one thing to plan a seduction in the abstract and quite another to put it into action when just looking at him turned her knees to jelly.

And it was just her luck that he was a triple threat kind of guy. First, he had a great body, strong and athletic. Second, he had a great mouth. It was better not to look at it too long. And then there were his eyes and the way he looked at her—as if he knew all her secrets and was just waiting for her to make a move so that he could counter it.

It made her want to do something, anything that he wouldn't expect.

That was the key. Drawing in a deep breath, she stiffened her spine. She had to think of something he wouldn't expect, something subtle, sneaky. The challenge sent a little ripple of anticipation through her.

"Hey, you two," Lucas said.

With a start, Sophie tore her eyes away from Tracker's and glanced at her brother. He and Mac had already started to make their way down the "aisle" formed by the guests.

"Stay close," Lucas continued, once he had their attention. "We're going right to the dance floor just as we did at the wedding."

Yes, Sophie decided as she walked with Tracker toward the platform that had been set up for dancing. A dance was a good start. And maybe an innocent little game...

A DANCE. That's all it was. Just a polite, social gesture—one of the many rituals that Lucas was determined to repeat for his bride. That's what Tracker told himself as he steered Sophie onto the dancing platform. It had been a year since he'd held the Princess in his arms, a year since he'd decided that he had to keep his distance from her. However much he thought he'd prepared himself, he couldn't prevent his body from hardening in anticipation of holding her, the reaction so automatic it was as if he had already been intimate with her.

And he had been very intimate with her in the fantasies that had fueled his dreams every night for the past year. A few of them flickered at the edge of his mind as the music began. Then her hand was in his, pressed palm to palm, and she raised the other one to rest on his shoulder. They touched nowhere else, but he could imagine her strong, slender fingers brushing over his skin, and flames licked along his nerve endings at the thought.

Fantasies were all he would ever have with Sophie Wainwright, Tracker reminded himself. Hardly a day went by that he didn't review the reasons why he'd resolved to steer clear of her. First off, she was his boss's sister—a boss who happened to be his best friend and the closest thing to family he'd ever known. Having an affair with Sophie Wainwright was out of the question. And anything else was impossible. They came from different worlds. Only in fairy tales did the princess and the knight who guarded her believe they might have anything more.

But she was close now, and each time the movements of the dance brought their bodies into contact, the hard knot of desire tightened inside of him. One thing was clear. He couldn't control his response to her any more than he'd been able to keep himself entirely away from her.

Lucas had asked him to keep an eye on her after the kidnapping. There were plenty of men Tracker could have assigned to watch over her. But he hadn't been able to give up watching over her himself.

That one simple fact worried him. Developing an iron-willed control over his emotions was one of the few things in his life he was proud of. His father had been a violent man, and Tracker knew that he'd inherited some of those tendencies. The work he'd done for the government had proved it. He couldn't allow anyone to get too close, especially not Sophie, who threatened his control as no woman ever had before.

Even now he couldn't seem to prevent himself from drawing her closer and torturing himself with the brush of her body against his. Each time she shifted, he felt the movement, along with an ache that began to grow deeper and sharper within him.

He wanted Sophie. To have her this close and not be able to take more was sheer torture.

"It's just not fair," Sophie said.

Her statement so clearly echoed his own thoughts

that for a second Tracker wondered if she could read his mind.

"What isn't fair?" he asked, glancing down. In that first moment of looking into those amber-colored eyes of hers, his mind went completely blank. All he could see, all he could absorb, was Sophie. She had the finest damn face—fair skinned, oval. This close, he could see what he never saw in his fantasies: there were flaws in that pale, almost translucent, skin. A sprinkle of freckles across her nose, the faintest scar on her chin... A man might be fooled into thinking she was delicate if he didn't notice the stubbornness in the strong line of her jaw.

Then his gaze fastened on her mouth. Her lips were parted, moist...and moving. He gave his head a quick shake to clear it when he realized she was talking to him.

"...agree with me?"

A short, balding man spun by, jostling against them and nearly losing the tall woman in his arms. For the first time, Tracker became aware that other couples had joined them on the dance floor. The beat of the music had picked up, too. How long had he been holding Sophie and fantasizing?

"Well, don't you?" she asked.

She was smiling at him. Tracker narrowed his eyes. The Princess didn't do that very often, and it made him wary. "Agree with you about what?"

"That it's simply not fair. You know everything about me, and I know next to nothing about you."

"You know everything you need to know about me."

Sophie shook her head. "I don't even know your real name. Lucas says you're called Tracker because in the service there wasn't anything you couldn't track. I don't know where you came from, either. Why don't we play a little game?"

Tracker frowned. "What kind of a game?"

"Oh, stop being so suspicious. I'm suggesting a game of twenty questions, and we'll take turns. You ask me a question and then I ask you one."

Tracker studied her as he steered her nearer the edge of the dance platform. He'd learned a lot about her when she'd donned a wig and led him on a merry chase cross-country last year, and she was definitely up to something. There was an unmistakable gleam of mischief in her eyes that he couldn't help but respond to. "What happens if I don't want to answer a particular question?"

"You can pass. But you have to pay a penalty, of course. Let's say…something simple to begin with…" Pausing, she tapped a finger on his chest. "I know. If you don't answer the question, the penalty is a kiss. What do you say? Are you game?"

No. He should say no. But his body was already on fire with the thought of lowering his mouth to hers, of taking just one taste. His hands had already gone to her waist. Her lips were only inches from his, and…

No. He should end this right now, simply set her aside and walk away. While he was trying to get his body to follow orders, she rose on her toes and her mouth was even closer. "I'll make it easy for you."

The whisper of her breath on his skin was nearly his undoing.

"You can go first. Ask me anything," she invited.

He couldn't imagine the snake in the Garden of Eden being any more persuasive. He could feel his blood draining from his head.

"I've got it. You've been following me all over Georgetown—every single time I've gone out with John Landry. I'll bet there's something you want to know about him—something that even you haven't been able to uncover. Wouldn't you like to know what my plans are so that you can tell Lucas? Aren't you wondering if I'm in love with him?"

"Are you in love with him?" The question slipped out before he could prevent it. It had been eating away at him like acid since she'd first started dating John Landry. Everything about the man had checked out. He came from wealth, the steady, deep-pocket kind that was handed down from one generation to another. His family tree was good, too; on his mother's side, he was related to an earl. Sophie had met him on one of her buying trips, and he was interested in antiques. In short, he was perfect for her. Tracker had told Lucas as much.

Sophie's lips curved into a smile. "I'm going to pass on that one."

"Pass?"

"I choose not to answer the question. So you can collect your penalty."

Now there was a mixture of amusement and recklessness in her eyes—and something else that had his body growing even harder. "You weren't going to answer any question I asked, were you?"

She grinned at him. "That's another question and

you haven't even collected the penalty for the first one. Unless…'' The challenge in her eyes was unmistakable. ''You're too much of a coward to collect?''

''You're playing with fire,'' he murmured as he tightened his arms around her and pressed her closer until their bodies were in contact from thigh to chest. He could have sworn that he felt her soften against him, one tantalizing degree at a time. The pulse at her throat fluttered frantically as he watched those incredible amber eyes darken and cloud.

Her response to him stirred him almost unbearably, and it occurred to him that he was the one playing with fire. Her mouth was barely an inch away, her lips parted and moist. His breath was already mingling with hers. One taste, just one, and perhaps he could satisfy the terrible hunger….

Later, he wasn't sure who closed the distance between them, but suddenly her mouth was brushing against his. For one second, he was sure that the floor shifted beneath his feet, and then the flood of sensations washed every thought out of his mind. Each one was so clear. Her hands burned his skin as they moved from his neck to his hair. Her teeth nipped at his bottom lip and then her tongue tangled with his. He'd dreamed so often of what her taste would be like. But it was different—much sweeter than he'd imagined. And the underlying hint of tartness reminded him of lemonade on a hot summer day. He'd never been able to drink enough of it to quench his thirst. A quick surge of desperation had him changing the angle of the kiss and taking it deeper. There were richer, riper flavors beneath her tongue, and he had to sample them all.

He had to touch her, too. In a quick possessive move, he ran his hands from her waist to the sides of her breasts. He'd waited forever to have his hands on her. She was so much softer than he'd fantasized. His mind clicked off and, instead of analyzing, became filled with the image of that slim, strong body beneath his, meeting him thrust for thrust.

DESPERATION. Sophie felt it in the hard grip of his hands and tasted it in the hard thrust of his tongue. Pleasure streamed through her in a series of sharp little explosions. And she wanted—no, she craved—more.

As a dream lover, he'd been gentle, caring—and he'd never taken her this far. Desire burned as hot and reckless as a bonfire out of control. Her heart pounded as if it might shoot right out of her chest. And her mind—it seemed as if the sensations pouring through her were causing it to short-circuit.

Questions spun in her head in random order. Why had she waited for a whole year to seduce him? Why had she chosen to do it on a dance floor in front of other people? Why, *why* didn't they go somewhere else fast?

Inching up even higher on her toes, she tightened her arms around his neck and shifted her hips against him. She felt the moan he gave in response in every pore of her body, and felt the hard press of his erection against her stomach. She was trying to get closer still when his hands gripped her wrists. He untangled her arms from around him, one then the other, and once he'd freed himself, he gently eased her away.

At first she was only aware of the coolness of the air on her skin and a sense of loss. She took a deep breath and found that her lungs were burning. And it didn't help one bit that Tracker was still looking at her as if he wanted nothing more than to devour her. "Why did you stop?"

"Damn it, Princess. Look around you."

The moment she did, reality flooded in. She'd completely forgotten that they were standing at the edge of the dance platform, barely an arm's length away from gyrating couples.

Someone cleared his throat. "Mind if I cut in?"

2

IT TOOK A MINUTE for the question to register in his mind, and another minute for Tracker to gather enough of his scattered wits to recognize the man who'd spoken: John Landry, the perfect match for Sophie Wainwright.

Yes, I mind. The words formed in his mind, but he managed to keep them from reaching his lips. He also managed to keep from shoving the man off the platform. Past Landry's shoulder, he could see couples were still dancing, and reality slipped fully into focus. One taste of Sophie and he'd nearly lost all control. He'd nearly taken her right on the dance floor. What had he been thinking?

"Sophie? Are you all right?" Landry asked.

Tracker glanced at her. She looked as shaken as he felt. More than anything, he wanted to reach out, draw her into his arms and just hold her. He might have if Landry hadn't reached out and taken her arm.

"Sophie." Mac nudged her way past two couples to join them. Giving Landry a quick smile, she said, "I'm so sorry to interrupt, but I need to borrow my maid of honor. Just a little fashion emergency. It won't take long." She shot an apologetic smile at both John

Landry and Tracker before she grabbed Sophie's hand and drew her off the dance floor.

Lucas was grinning from ear to ear as he joined the two men. "Mac needs a little help with her wardrobe. Shouldn't take long, Landry. Then Sophie will be all yours."

Over my dead body. The thought sprang to Tracker's mind before he could stifle it. He hoped to God that he hadn't said it out loud.

"No problem," John Landry said. "I'll just help myself to a drink."

Tracker kept his eyes on the man until he was off the dance floor.

"I sense a little hostility in the air," Lucas said. "Mac and I are happy that Sophie is dating again, but if you've discovered something about Landry I should know…"

Tracker studied his friend, but there wasn't any sign that Lucas had seen him kiss Sophie. *Good,* he told himself. The kiss had been a mistake—one he wasn't going to repeat. "No. Landry's background checks out. There's nothing to show that he's after Sophie's money."

Jealousy had a bitter, coppery taste, Tracker discovered. Landry was the perfect man for Sophie; he wasn't. That simple fact had been a lot easier to live with before he'd kissed her. Ruthlessly, he shoved the memory aside. "Mac looks fine. What's the emergency?"

Lucas leaned closer. "She has to change because she just popped a button on her skirt. The baby's growing."

Tracker studied his friend. There was no mistaking the pride in his voice or the joy in his eyes. A stab of envy pierced him. "You hit the jackpot, didn't you?"

"Yeah." Lucas threw an arm around Tracker's shoulders. "C'mon, let's go into my study for a minute and we can drink to that. Plus, I have a surprise—an old friend you and I haven't seen for a long time."

"THERE, I might look like I'm wearing pajamas, but I feel much better." Mac pressed her hands against her rounding stomach as she studied herself in the full-length mirror. She'd changed from her two-piece evening gown into a white silk pantsuit in a stretchy fabric.

"You look beautiful," Sophie said. "And you have no need to worry that your husband is going to develop a wandering eye just because you're having a baby. He's totally besotted with you."

"It's mutual." Mac smiled as tears began to fill her eyes. "And I'm not worried. He's throwing this party and taking me back to the island where we spent our honeymoon to let me know that even though I look like a blimp, nothing has changed—he'll be with me forever."

Sophie felt a knot of envy tighten in her stomach.

"No one has ever done anything like that for me," Mac continued. "And I have you to thank for it. If you hadn't pushed me into using my research on Lucas last year..."

Taking Tracker's handkerchief from her evening bag, Sophie handed it to Mac. "Yeah, well, my motives were not entirely altruistic."

Sophie remembered quite clearly how she'd felt at the time, fresh from the humiliation of having her brother and Tracker McBride prove to her that her fiancé was only interested in her money. "I used you. I was more than a little annoyed at Lucas, and I thought having you practice your sexual fantasy research on him would get me out from under his constant surveillance." Plus, it had given her great pleasure to outwit Tracker McBride.

Mac took Sophie's hands. "You insisted that I use Lucas as a guinea pig to test my research on sexual fantasies because you didn't want me to practice them on a stranger. Not only that, when I wanted to cut and run, you gave me the courage to stick it out. You were my role model. And I owe you for that."

"That's nonsense," Sophie said. "You and Lucas were made for each other."

Mac shook her head. "Being meant for each other isn't enough. Take it from an expert on the subject. I wouldn't be here today if you hadn't nudged me into flying out to that island in your place. The last thing Lucas was looking for was a relationship. And I wasn't even the type he preferred to date. He told me that he'd decided never to marry." Mac waved a hand. "I wouldn't have all this if you hadn't badgered me until I worked up the courage to tell Lucas just why I was there."

"Mac, I—" Embarrassed, Sophie tried to pull her hands away, but Mac held tight.

"No. I'm going to finish this. It's my turn to nudge you. I saw you kissing Tracker on the dance floor."

Everyone must have seen them. "I...that is, we..."

She hadn't let herself think about the kiss since Mac had led her off the dance floor. When Sophie had started the game, she certainly hadn't expected it to go as far as it had. She'd forgotten everything—the game, her plan, everything but Tracker. "You must be thinking…"

"I'm thinking it's about time you made a move on him."

Sophie blinked. "Really?"

"Since he's one of the most self-disciplined and self-contained men I've ever met, I think you were wise to take the initiative. I'm dying to know what you did to get him to kiss you."

Sophie let out a dry laugh. "Would you believe I asked him to play a game of twenty questions, and the penalty for not answering a question was a kiss?"

"What a great idea," Mac said with delight, reaching for a small notepad on the nightstand. "I don't think I have an example of that in my research. Twenty questions," she murmured as she scribbled on the pad.

"Yeah, well, you better add a warning that the game is best played in private."

Mac glanced up. "He's that good a kisser, huh?"

Sophie nodded. "I'm pretty sure some of my brain cells died. I couldn't even feel my legs when I followed you off of the dance floor. And if Tracker hadn't all of a sudden ended it, I would have…" A vivid image of exactly what she might have done formed in her mind. "Mac, you might have had an X-rated incident right in the middle of your anniversary party."

Mac threw back her head and laughed, and in a moment, Sophie joined her. By the time they could both breathe again, they had settled on the edge of the bed.

"I don't know why I'm laughing," Sophie said. "Tracker will probably have disappeared again by the time I get back downstairs."

"I don't think so," Mac said. "There's something between the two of you. I can see it whenever you're in the same room together."

"Well, that doesn't happen often. He avoids me like the plague. And when he's forced into my company, he treats me like a kid sister."

"Not tonight. And he *never* looks at you like a man looks at his sister. Tracker looks at you like he wants to throw you over his shoulder and carry you off somewhere. And he talks about you, you know."

Sophie met Mac's eyes. "He does?"

She nodded. "He thinks you're one of the bravest women he's ever known. And the smartest."

Sophie knew that Tracker was a frequent visitor at Mac and Lucas's house in Georgetown, but he never visited when she was there.

"I've seen the way you look at him, too," Mac said. "After that kiss, you can't tell me you're not interested in him, or that you don't lust after him, at least."

Sophie drew in a deep breath. "To tell you the truth, I've been toying with the idea of having an affair with him. But he's so…intimidating. I think I have a plan—but then he looks at me and my brains cells start to leak. I'm going to need more than a game of twenty questions with penalties."

Mac beamed a smile at her as she rose and moved to her dresser. "I have just the thing. In fact, I put some items together as a little first-anniversary gift, bride to maid of honor. I was going to give this to you anyway, since you've started dating again. But I'm much more comfortable knowing that you'll use them on Tracker. He has a weakness for games—especially games of chance."

"He does?" Sophie looked curiously at the small bag Mac was lifting off the dresser.

Nodding, she sat back down on the bed and reached into the bag. "I was thinking of Tracker when I selected these items. Must have been ESP or something. There, I've got it." She held out a coin to Sophie.

"A quarter?"

"A two-headed quarter. I had a few good times using it with Lucas—until he figured it out."

Sophie took the coin and examined it. Her mind was already racing with ideas as she glanced back at Mac. "You are a continual surprise to me."

Mac beamed a smile at her as she pulled out a giant-size pair of dice. "Lucas says the same thing."

Sophie stared at the dice. Instead of numbers, there were words printed on the sides. One die named actions: stroke, lick, kiss. The other named body parts: back, neck, breasts.

"They're a lot of fun," Mac said.

Sophie turned the stuffed dice over in her hands. "Any way you roll them, it looks like a win-win situation to me. Where did you get them?"

"My friend in Paris told me about this great Web site." She drew a final item out of the bag.

"A deck of cards?" Sophie asked.

"They *look* like playing cards," Mac said as she fanned them open. "But they're really coupons."

Sophie drew one. "'This card entitles you to a *quickie* on demand. You name the time and place.'"

"You give it to the person and it's up to them to decide where and when to demand the quickie. I pick riskier places than Lucas does. It throws him off balance."

Sophie grinned. "You're so good for him, Mac."

"You'll be good for Tracker, too. He's lonely."

She'd never thought of Tracker as having any vulnerabilities.

"He probably needs a little encouragement. Lucas did. And some of these little toys get amazing results."

Sophie picked up the final item that Mac took out of the bag, a black velvet ribbon, and drew it through her fingers. "What kind of game do you play with this?"

Mac tilted her head to one side. "Bondage comes to mind, but there's a tag with an interesting suggestion."

Sophie glanced at the tag and saw that it even included a diagram with what she suspected was a highly inventive Kama Sutra position. The man was seated, the woman was on his lap—backward—and the ribbon was looped around his... Tilting the card sideways, Sophie narrowed her eyes. Yep, the ribbon was looped around exactly what she'd thought. "Are you sure this is anatomically possible?"

Mac cleared her throat. "Not from personal experience. I think you have to have great powers of concentration to actually... My advice would be to improvise."

Sophie glanced around the bed at the sex toys that Mac had taken out of the gift bag. "I'm getting that message loud and clear."

"Tracker would be a safe person to try these out on."

Safe. Yes. In spite of his air of mystery and danger, she'd never felt safer than when Tracker had held her in his arms that very first day in Lucas's office. Right after she'd punched her brother.

"Go for it, Sophie."

"TRACKER, I'd like you to meet Carter Mitchell," Lucas said as he closed the French doors leading to the patio, and strode into his office. "He's one of the two men Sophie brought this evening."

Tracker recognized the name. Carter Mitchell was the manager of the art gallery next door to Sophie's shop. Since Mitchell's relationship with Sophie had been strictly business, Tracker had had one of his men run a routine check. Now Tracker caught something familiar in the way Mitchell moved as he rose from his chair. The face was familiar, too. Although it was leaner now and harder, there were still traces of the baby-faced twenty-two-year-old he and Lucas had worked with on their last mission six years ago.

"Chance?" he said, narrowing his eyes as he took in the Italian designer suit, the slim gold bracelet he wore on one wrist and the diamond earring in his left ear. Chance had been the only name he'd known this man by when they'd worked together. They'd called him that because there wasn't a chance that he wouldn't take.

"Yeah." He stepped toward Tracker and extended

his hand. "I figured I'd have to come clean the moment I walked through that door with Sophie. The name's Carter Mitchell now."

Lucas moved to stand behind his desk. "Seems our old friend Chance is working undercover and he wants to make sure we don't spoil things for him."

There was a steeliness in Lucas's voice that had Tracker withdrawing his hand from Chance's grasp.

"He took me aside and asked me not to give away his cover," Lucas said. Then he turned to Chance. "Now, I want an uncut, uncensored version of who you're working for, and if my sister is involved."

"I work for a group of insurance companies that want to recover some stolen artifacts from an archeological find in Turkey, most importantly three rare coins. They were in England when they were stolen, and it's caused quite an international stir. Various investigative agencies including Interpol and the feds have concluded that the stuff's being brought into this country cleverly concealed in shipments to selected commercial locations. Sophie's shop had been identified as warranting close surveillance."

"How long has she been a target of the investigation?" Lucas asked.

"For about a month and a half. That's when I became the new manager of the art gallery next to her shop. A month ago we got our first big break in the case. An operative on this side got close enough to the head guy to actually buy a piece we believe contained one of the coins. She purchased it at One of a Kind, and she was supposed to deliver it in person to her boss."

"Supposed to?" Tracker's eyes narrowed.

"Five minutes after she left the shop, she was the victim of a hit-and-run driver. Two men came out of nowhere. One pushed her into an oncoming car, the other took the package and then both ran."

"And you've waited a month to let me know my sister might be in mortal danger?"

Chance switched his gaze to Lucas. "I swear I didn't put Sophie together with you until I walked in here tonight. None of us went by our real names when we worked together. Hell, I didn't even know you had a sister."

Everything Chance said was true enough. The kind of operations they'd worked on never appeared in the newspapers, and real names were never mentioned.

"And now you've decided to date her?" Tracker asked, silently cursing himself. He'd focused his time and the time of his staff checking out the men Sophie went out with even casually. If she'd gone out with Chance sooner, he'd have had a photo of the man standing in front of him, and he'd have known over a month ago that something was up.

Once again, Chance raised his hands, but this time he grinned. "Hey, I'm not her date tonight. I'm just her tag-along gay friend."

"You're *not* gay," Tracker said.

Chance shrugged. "It's part of my cover. Telling a woman you're gay is the quickest way to lower barriers short of taking her to bed—and that's a little complicated if she's one of your prime suspects."

For a moment, Tracker didn't say a word. He had to get a grip. Anger wasn't going to help—nor was fear. "Sophie's not involved in smuggling anything."

"I eliminated her as soon as I got to know her. She doesn't have a dishonest bone in her body. And she loves that shop of hers too much to risk it by getting involved in something like this." Chance's eyes narrowed and grew colder. "But someone on this side is funneling the goods to the right person."

"Do you suspect Noah Danforth, her assistant?" Lucas asked.

"It could be him," Chance replied. "Or it could be any one of her regular customers. She makes them feel like family. All it would take was a word that they were looking for a particular piece, and she'd see that it was set aside. Noah would do the same."

"So the only thing you really know is that anyone who gets close to the head guy ends up dead." Lucas turned to Tracker. "I want her out of that shop until the investigation is over."

"That won't necessarily keep her safe," Chance said quickly. "Whoever is behind this is very clever. His nickname is 'Puppet Master' because he stays in the background and just pulls the strings. We got close to him three months ago when he shipped the first of the coins. He used a small shop in Connecticut, and the owner was killed in a fire that destroyed his shop. If this guy gets even a hint that Sophie knows anything, she could still be in mortal danger. The only way to really keep her safe is to find out who's behind this."

Tracker paced to the French doors. The hell of it was Chance was making sense. From the sounds of it, the bastard behind the smuggling ring didn't leave any loose ends that could be traced back to him.

"I'll cancel my trip," Lucas said.

"No." Tracker turned to face him. "If you do, Sophie will know something is wrong. And so will Mac."

"It should all be over in the next week," Chance said. "Sophie has a shipment due in tomorrow, and the last of the three coins is supposed to be on it. Together, they're worth more than they are apart. We're pretty sure that the first coin went to the shop in Connecticut. The second one was picked up by the woman who was hit and killed after she left Sophie's store. I've already offered to help Sophie unpack the delivery and arrange the pieces in the shop. Whoever is behind this will move quickly. All we have to do is trace the piece containing the coin to the buyer, and we'll have our man."

Through the glass of the French doors, Tracker's eyes went unerringly to one couple on the dance floor. Sophie was dancing with John Landry. Silently, he cursed himself. He'd missed Sophie's growing friendship with the gallery owner, Carter Mitchell. What had he overlooked in her relationship with John Landry?

"What about this Landry fellow?" Tracker asked. "Sophie met him on her last trip to England."

"He's clean. I checked him out myself."

Tracker turned back to Lucas. "I'll be there, too, when she unpacks the shipment."

"How? You can't do anything to alert her to what's going on. The worst thing that could happen is for her to start acting strangely with Danforth or her customers," Chance warned.

"I won't alert her," Tracker promised.

"She's not an easy woman to fool," Lucas said.

"I'll figure something out," Tracker said. "And she'll never suspect a thing." Then he turned back to Chance. "Right now I want you to fill me in on everything, including a list of your top suspects."

3

SOPHIE HATED DUMPING anyone. She'd suffered enough rejection in her own life to know how much it hurt. But she ran the risk of hurting John Landry even more if she wasn't honest with him. That's what she'd been telling herself as she'd avoided him for the two hours since she'd left Mac's bedroom. But even now, dancing with him, she was putting off the inevitable moment.

"Sophie?"

"Hmm?" It didn't help one bit that she could feel Tracker's gaze on the back of her neck. She hadn't actually seen him since she and Mac had left the dance floor hours ago, but now the tension that she felt whenever he was near was back in full force. He was watching her dance with John Landry. The certainty of that gave her spirits a little lift, and she was very tempted to give him something to watch. But she couldn't flirt with John Landry—or kiss him—and *then* dump him.

Besides, all she could think of was kissing Tracker again. She had to know if lightning could strike twice. Her mind drifted back to the time she'd spent with Mac in the bedroom. Those toys. Just thinking about using them with Tracker sent a wave of heat rushing through Sophie.

First she had to come up with a plan to get him within using distance. And she'd have to get him very close to use that black ribbon.

"Sophie?"

"Hmm?" She glanced up to find John Landry frowning down at her. Had he been talking to her?

"Sophie, your body is here dancing with me, but your mind is a million miles away."

No, not a million. She figured it was about fifty yards to the French doors where Tracker was standing, watching her. And she wasn't being fair to John.

"I want you to come with me to my hotel," he murmured. "Leave your car here and I'll drive you back to get it tomorrow."

She drew in a deep breath. She'd insisted on bringing her own car because she'd known she wouldn't be returning with John. "I'm sorry. I can't."

"I'll follow you, then. I want time with you. Alone."

"John." With a quick look around, she took his hand and led him off the dance floor toward the shelter of some trees, where they could have a little privacy. "I'm sorry, but I'm not going to spend time with you alone—the way you mean it. I…" For a moment she thought she saw a flash of anger in his eyes, but it was masked so quickly that she might have been mistaken.

"I don't mean to rush you," he said.

"It's not that you're rushing me," she said. "I think you've been very patient, but I don't think that I'll change my mind with time. And I'm sorry if I led you on. You're such a nice man, and I value you as a friend and a business colleague." Sophie stopped then because she felt little prickles of awareness along her nerve endings. Tracker was near. He was listening to every word she said.

"Well," John said, and then cleared his throat. "I won't tell you that I didn't hope for more. But I value your friendship also, enough so that I won't jeopardize it by pushing you further than you want to go. But I do want to see you again, strictly for business. You've aroused my curiosity about that shipment you're receiving tomorrow."

Sophie smiled at him. "I'll expect you at the shop bright and early. And I'll put you to work unloading it."

"Good." He took her hands and squeezed them. "I'll see you tomorrow."

As he turned and walked away toward the front of the house, Sophie took one step after him, wanting to say something more.

"I wouldn't," said a low voice, so close that she jumped. "It's always best to make a clean break."

She turned to see Tracker separate himself from the shadow of the trees. "It's rude to eavesdrop."

He moved closer then, and it was all she could do not to take a quick step back at the overwhelming effect of his proximity.

"If you wanted your conversation to be private, you shouldn't have had it in a garden. Besides, when you're going to dump guys, it's good to have someone close by. They think twice before they get violent."

"John Landry is a very nice man. He would never get violent." She thought of the flash of anger she'd seen in his eyes.

"Take it from me, he was pissed." Tracker grinned at her. "You're lucky he's such a *nice* guy."

Sophie narrowed her eyes. She didn't like the way he'd said "nice" as if it meant wimp. "There's nothing wrong with being nice."

"Right." Tracker's chuckle was deep and so infectious that for a moment she wanted nothing more than to join him. She stifled the impulse.

"When was the last time being nice got you what you wanted in this world?" he asked.

Well, that was true enough, she thought. And hadn't she already decided that being *nice* wasn't going to get her very far with him, either? He probably preferred naughty over nice twenty-four–seven. The idea sent a little thrill running through her.

"Being nice didn't get Landry what he wanted."

It occurred to her that this was the longest conversation she'd ever had with Tracker McBride. "And your suggestion to him would be?"

His expression sobered and he met her eyes directly. "If he wants you, he should reach out and take you."

The words, combined with the look he gave her, were enough to tighten all the muscles deep inside of her.

She lifted her chin. "And just what do *you* want?"

For a moment he said nothing. Then he smiled slowly, and she felt her knees go weak. "Me? I'm just going to do my job and follow you home."

So they were back to that, were they? Temper stiffened her spine. "I don't need an escort."

"Look, Princess, it's late, both of your dates have driven home in their own cars, and Lucas doesn't want you going home alone.'' Tracker waited a beat and then continued. ''You'll just waste your energy if you try to lose me. Don't expect to play that little game again and win.''

Although it cost her, she said nothing. Five years in business had taught her that keeping her temper was crucial if she wanted to sell a customer on her way of thinking. And her way of thinking—until he'd annoyed her by reminding her that he was her guardian angel—was to get Tracker within touching distance. If he followed her to her apartment, all she had to do was get him inside.

She tilted her head at him. ''Relax, Tracker. I'm not going to run away again. That game bores me. I'd much rather continue the one we started on the dance floor.''

His eyes narrowed, but he said nothing.

''Why don't we leave it up to chance?'' Reaching into her pocket, she pulled out the coin Mac had given her. ''A simple toss of the coin. Heads, you come up when we get to my place and we continue our game of twenty questions. Tails, you follow me home and slide back into the shadows. Are you game?''

He studied her for a moment. ''Okay. Toss the coin.''

She tossed it up, caught it and let him look. ''Heads. And since it's my turn to ask a question, I'll tell you what it is so you can think about it. I want to know what your real name is.''

Pocketing the coin, she turned and headed toward her car. Let him chew on that while he followed her home.

WHAT IN HELL KIND OF GAME was she playing? The question had been plaguing him ever since the Princess had flipped that damn coin. Easing his foot off the gas, he allowed the car to drop back a little farther behind Sophie's as they sped along the expressway that would take them into the District of Columbia. The last thing he was going to do was crowd her. She'd surprised him three times tonight. First of all, she'd kissed him. Then she'd dumped Landry. And now she'd invited Tracker into her apartment for a continuation of their game of twenty questions. He didn't like surprises where the Princess was concerned, especially when the stakes were this high.

Since he couldn't predict what kind of game she was playing, he'd make sure the odds were in his favor.

When she slowed and signaled a turn onto an offramp, he eased his foot from the gas.

He should never have kissed her on the dance floor. He hadn't been able to resist her. And that one kiss had confirmed his worst suspicion: *one* was not going to be enough with Sophie Wainright. Not nearly. Whatever he'd imagined in his fantasies hadn't come close to reality. One taste and his control had slipped. The pull between them was so elemental that before he'd found the strength to set her away, he'd lost something of himself.

He wanted her, and he was beginning to understand that he would have her. The need he had for her might not leave him with any choice. The thought chilled him even as it made every pulse in his body throb. But for now—tonight and the next few days—he had a job to do, and he would do it much better if he could maintain some distance.

Pressing his foot on the accelerator, he closed the distance between them. It was time for plan A. Uncapping the bottle he'd pulled from his pocket, he took a good swallow. It would take about five minutes for the contents to work its magic on his stomach.

He planned to spend the night in Sophie's apartment, but *not* in her bed. Tonight, he wasn't going to take any chances. He hadn't kept watch over the Princess for two years without figuring out what her weaknesses were, and she was a sucker for strays and under-dogs.

When the first stomach cramp hit, he closed the distance between the cars and let his weave all the way onto the shoulder. Slamming on the brakes, he made sure the tires made plenty of noise on the gravel before he came to a complete stop. Then he stumbled out of the car and emptied his stomach on the grass verge.

If he knew the Princess, just pretending to be sick wasn't going to work. She was going to need to see the evidence, and there it was. One of his foster mothers had introduced him to the curative powers of ipecac when he'd gotten into her medicine cabinet. He kept a bottle in the kit with his other ''tools.''

Leaning against the fender, weaker than he'd thought he would be, he watched Sophie gun her car backward along the shoulder until she screeched to a halt about five feet in front of him. She was out of the car and running toward him so fast that watching her brought on another wave of nausea. He pressed a hand against his stomach.

"What happened? Are you all right?"

The concern in her eyes was everything he'd hoped for. Plan A was going to work just fine.

"It must have been something I ate."

When she glanced past him at the grass, he tried to block her view after he was sure she'd seen the evidence.

Her eyes narrowed. "Are you drunk?"

He shook his head and felt another wave of nausea hit. This one had him doubling over, and his deposit just missed her opened-toed sandals. He was beginning to think he'd taken too big a dose.

"C'mon. I'll drive. You're in no condition to operate a vehicle. You can send one of your men to pick up your car later."

"I didn't drink too much. It was the food," he protested as she opened the passenger door and settled him inside. Before she got the door shut, he leaned out and made another deposit on the grass.

Without a word, she closed the door, marched around to get in the driver's side. Plan A might have a few minor bumps that had to be ironed out, but he figured he was halfway there when she started the car.

"Sorry about this. I think I just need some sleep," he said as they pulled back onto the highway. It had been more than twenty years since his foster mom had dosed him, and he didn't recall feeling this sleepy afterward. Nor had his head felt quite this heavy. He tried to clear his mind. "T.J."

"What?" Sophie sent him a sideways glance.

"My name. It's T.J. Next question's mine."

"Not on your life," she said. "Initials don't count.

I want your real name, or a penalty. But let's get you back on your feet first.''

It wouldn't hurt to pretend to sleep, he decided. That should be enough to get the Princess to take him home with her.

THE NEXT THING Tracker knew, someone was nudging his shoulder.

''Time to wake up.''

''Hmm? Where are we?'' Opening his eyes, he blinked against the lights.

''We're at the hospital.''

He came fully awake and saw that Sophie had pulled the car into the well-lit entrance of a hospital emergency room. ''I'm not going in there.''

''Afraid of hospitals, are we?''

''No. I just don't need one.''

''Relax,'' she said as she climbed out of the driver's seat and walked around the front of the car. ''Don't worry about a thing.''

Damn, he'd underestimated her nurturing instinct. And she had him between a rock and a hard place. If he told her he wasn't really sick, he'd ruin plan A. While he mulled over what to do, she opened the car door.

''I told you I was fine,'' he said.

''C'mon, I'll hold your hand while they examine you,'' she assured him as she helped him out of the car.

Shit, he thought. By the time they released him, he'd sure as hell better come up with Plan B.

"REPORT," the man said as he pressed the button on the speakerphone. Then he leaned forward to adjust the position of one of his knights on the chessboard.

"Everything is going according to plan."

"Not quite," said the man.

There was a beat of silence. He let it stretch to two beats and then three. "Your plan was to become her lover so that you would be intimate with her when the shipment arrived. She left the party with another man."

"I'll be at the shop when the coin arrives tomorrow."

"But you'll have company. He's in her apartment right now, and perhaps in her bed, where you were supposed to be."

"I'll handle it."

"You know the penalty if you don't."

Replacing the receiver, the man leaned back in his chair and studied the reaction of his companion.

"I can handle him. Just give me the word, and I'll have him out of the way."

"Such ruthlessness," the man admonished. He would discourage it now, but it would come in handy later. He took a sip of his brandy. "Patience, my friend. This particular puppet may still be of some use. Besides, removing him now might draw too much attention to Ms. Wainwright's shop, and we don't have the coin yet."

The man called the Puppet Master had other puppets in place. Any one of them could get the coin tomorrow, and his companion would be useful later. His long-term success lay in knowing how to play the game.

He would wait, for now. The coin would be here tomorrow and once he had it, he would have all three.

"Your move." He smiled and gestured toward the chessboard.

4

TRACKER AWOKE to find a rather large, tiger-striped cat sleeping on his chest. In the time it took him to remove the creature and set it on the floor, his mind cleared and the events of the previous evening came flooding back.

The side trip to the emergency room had turned out better than he'd expected. After a two-hour wait, they'd finally been escorted to a sheet-draped cubicle where an exhausted-looking doctor had ventured a diagnosis of mild food poisoning and pronounced Tracker good to go. By that time, he'd fully recovered from any lingering effects of the ipecac he'd taken, and he'd managed to charm one of the nurses into suggesting to Sophie that she keep him under surveillance for another forty-eight hours.

As a result, his game plan was back on track: he was exactly where he wanted to be, a recovering invalid in the Princess's apartment.

Swinging his feet to the floor, Tracker sat up and glanced around the narrow living room. It had surprised him. Sophie had been raised in a mansion, and she'd chosen to live in a place that wasn't much larger than a cell. He knew she had the convenience of living adjacent to her shop by residing here, but it was no palace for a princess.

The most surprising thing was that the room didn't seem cramped. It was…comfortable. The honey-colored, pegged-wood floor wasn't broken by rugs, but ran in a smooth line to the counter separating the rest of the living area from the kitchen. Aside from the overstuffed white sofa he'd spent the night on, and the cherub-faced jockey standing guard by the door, the room seemed almost monastic in its furnishings. But the bright explosion of color in the paintings that hung on the wall brought a homey warmth to the room. One on the opposite wall drew his eye. Pansies in every possible shade of red splattered across the canvas. It made him think of passion, hot and reckless, and of Sophie.

Dragging his eyes from it, he forced his gaze to the wall behind the couch and stared at the collection of horses. He hadn't noticed them last night. All in all, he figured the shelves held nearly fifty equestrian figures, some cast in clay, others carved of wood or marble.

So, the Princess loved horses. He tucked the knowledge away.

"Mmmrph."

Tracker glanced down to see that the cat had jumped back up on the couch. "You're Chess, right?"

The cat blinked and stared.

Sophie had introduced them when they'd arrived. Then she'd given Tracker a quick tour, showing him the bathroom, which was half the size of the living room and had doors that accessed both the living room and the bedroom.

She hadn't shown him her bedroom. If she had, he might have been with her in that bed right now. He didn't kid himself that it was going to be easy sticking to his game plan. And the Princess might have some plans of her own. He was going to have to keep his guard up and his wits about him.

Just thinking about matching wits with her made him smile. He hadn't felt this alive since he'd followed her across the country last year. Had he been waiting all this time for her to challenge him again?

"Mmmrmph."

He glanced down at the cat. "Hungry?"

The question had Chess sliding onto his lap.

Scooping him up, Tracker moved to the kitchen, located cat food and filled one of Chess's dishes. The other he filled with water. The cat dug in.

Satisfying his own hunger was going to be more problematic. Oh, the pantry was well stocked and he'd found eggs and butter in the refrigerator, bacon and coffee beans in the freezer. He might have fixed the Princess breakfast in bed if it weren't for two problems.

First, he was supposed to be recovering from food poisoning. Second, going into Sophie's bedroom for any reason would trigger a different and more basic kind of hunger.

Basic was a good word for it. Tracker was beginning to believe that having the Princess was becoming every bit as necessary to him as breathing. From that first day in Lucas's office, when he'd held her in his arms, he hadn't been able to break free of the hold she had on him.

In the middle of last night, she'd come out to check on him, and he'd used every bit of control he had to lie still and pretend to be asleep. Then he'd spent the rest of the night fantasizing what it would have been like to have her beneath him on that couch.

He had a job to do, he reminded himself. And he needed a clear head to do it.

When the cat jumped onto the counter, Tracker scratched him under his chin. "I might not be able to manage breakfast, but coffee might be a good idea. And then a cold shower. What do you think, Chess?"

The cat growled deep in his throat.

COFFEE. The scent of it had Sophie drifting up out of her dream. It had to be a dream, she thought as she sat up and shoved the hair out of her eyes. She was never organized enough to fill the coffeepot and set the automatic timer before she went to bed.

The second breath she inhaled told her she wasn't dreaming. And the memories flooded in. Tracker McBride had spent the night in her apartment. He'd made coffee in her kitchen.

Okay, so he wasn't in her bed yet. But she was making progress. She'd very nearly hugged the blond, perky nurse at the hospital who'd strongly urged that she keep Tracker under surveillance for at least twenty-four—preferably forty-eight—hours. And the wait in the emergency room had given her a lot of time to analyze the situation and to plan.

Sitting up, she plumped the pillows behind her and

pressed a hand to her stomach. There was no reason for it to be so jumpy. She could do this. After all, she had the coin. A quick glance at the nightstand assured her that it was still where she'd left it. And the little bag with Mac's ''toys'' was right at the side of her bed.

Lifting it, she drew out the black velvet ribbon that lay on top. She was going to have to work up a lot of nerve to use something like this. Truth be told, her confidence with men was mostly a sham. She could count on one hand the lovers she'd had, and most of them had been…unimaginative. Or maybe it had been her.

Well, with a little help from Mac's toys, Sophie was about to become a new woman.

When she heard the shower start, a little skip of panic moved up her spine. She'd better hurry and examine her plan because she was going to have to put it into action soon. Slipping out of bed, she grabbed her robe and tucked the coin into her pocket.

The key to any good business deal was to offer the other party exactly what he or she wanted. She and Tracker wanted each other, and so she would offer him a no-strings affair. What could be more simple or basic than that?

She began to pace. She'd have to take the first step. In spite of that kiss, he hadn't made any move to touch her once they'd entered her apartment.

When she was making a sale in her shop, timing was everything. And surprise. If she could catch him off guard, she would have the advantage.

She was lifting Mac's bag of toys off the bed when the sound of the shower stopped. An image filled her mind of Tracker stepping out of the tub, water dripping from him. A river of heat pooled in her center. She could picture him so clearly—lean muscles, long bones and taut, slick skin. Even as the bag slipped through her fingers, she was moving toward the bathroom door. Timing. Surprise.

Gripping the handle, she turned it and found it locked. No. *No.* She pounded on the door. ''Tracker!''

The lock clicked, the door flew open and she saw him. His scent—it assaulted her with its potency. His heat—she felt it reaching out to her, touching her. All thoughts of perfect timing and surprise drained from her mind as her body went into sensory overload. She was so aware of him, all at once, that she felt paralyzed. His skin was slick and damp—and only part of it was covered by the towel. Lust—a quick, sharp slap of it—filled her, along with greed. She wanted—no, she *needed*—to touch him, to run her hands over every inch of him.

And she would, just as soon as she could move her arms.

For a moment, Tracker stood absolutely still, paralyzed by a swift onslaught of emotions. When she'd called his name, fear had hit him hard, like a sucker punch to his gut. In the three short seconds that it had taken him to open the door to her bedroom, he'd realized that he hadn't checked it out. Last night, he hadn't trusted himself to even set foot in the room. Someone could have gotten in through a fire escape or through a back entrance to the apartment.

Though his eyes never left Sophie, he instantly catalogued the room, taking in a tall dresser, a full-length oval mirror, a bed. The closet door, standing ajar.

She was alone in the room. Safe.

He had about one second to process relief before he was sucker-punched by pure lust.

The oval-shaped mirror stood at an angle behind her, so that he could see her back and front. Her robe was a thin bit of silk and lace that draped over her breasts and hips so closely that it made a man wonder if she wore anything beneath. The thought of touching her and finding out had his blood running hotly, greedily.

It took every bit of strength he had not to tumble her onto the bed. He could have her just that quickly, and put an end to the desire that was clawing at his insides.

"Are you all right?" His voice sounded strained, raw.

"I thought you'd gone."

He should go. He should step back into the bathroom and relock the door. She was fine. He'd overreacted to a false alarm. And if he didn't get control of the situation, he wouldn't be prepared when a real alarm sounded. He ordered himself to back out of the room right now. But he didn't move. And he wasn't going to. His feet had stopped taking orders from his brain.

"I'm not going anywhere."

"Good." She moistened her lips, and Tracker had to swallow a moan. "I don't want you to go. I wanted to talk."

Talk? The woman was killing him.

TALK? What was she saying? Sophie wanted to jump him. But she couldn't seem to make her body take orders. She couldn't even remember the little speech she'd been rehearsing before she'd decided to storm the bathroom. The ripe, hot desire she saw in his eyes was melting her brain. She wasn't even sure she *could* talk.

Taking a deep breath, she gave it a try. "I want to make love to you." She might have turned around to see who'd spoken if she could have taken her eyes off Tracker. The good news was that his gaze was still hot enough to burn her skin. The bad news was he wasn't moving.

You can do this, Sophie. You're Mac's role model. "Right now would be good for me. Are you game?"

There was a beat of silence, his eyes never leaving hers. She saw his jaw tighten as he clenched his teeth. "It's not that I don't want you."

But. He hadn't said it, but the word threatened to slam down between them like a brick wall. Panic bubbled up at the same moment that her fingers closed around the coin in her pocket. Thank heavens her fingers were working. Testing, she took a step toward him. She could move. She could do this. "The way I see it, we could have a debate about the pros and cons, but why don't we cut right to the chase and settle it with a coin toss?"

Taking the quarter out of her pocket, she tossed it into the air. "Heads, we make love. Tails, we…"

TRACKER WATCHED THE COIN sail into the air. It didn't matter which way it came down, they were going to make love. He'd lost whatever battle he'd been waging with himself the moment she'd said, "I want to make love to you."

He hadn't expected it, hadn't built up any defense against the possibility.

How could he have possibly known that it was the one thing he'd wanted to hear her say? From the moment he'd heard those words, he'd wanted her on that bed beneath him, and he didn't know how much longer he could wait.

"Heads," she said as she glanced down at the coin and then held it out for him to see. "Okay, that's settled."

Fear gripped him then. In a second he was going to touch her, and he had to make sure that he maintained control. He'd pay a price for making love to her, but he had to make sure that she didn't. He didn't want to hurt her, and the urge to take her swiftly was so huge.

"Unless you'd rather...talk? Set up some ground rules?" She fumbled a little, slipping the coin into her pocket, and he noticed for the first time that her hands were trembling.

Nerves. He'd always thought of her as the Princess, so confident, so brave. That she was nervous because of him thrilled him and softened something inside of him. Tracker wasn't even aware that he'd closed the remaining distance between them until he touched her shoulders and absorbed the quick shiver that moved through her.

"Easy." He ran his hands slowly up and down her

arms the way he might gentle one of his horses. Then, lifting her hand, he pressed his lips to her palm, and watched the pulse at her throat quicken. "We'll talk later. Right now, I want to make love to you."

She moved her hands to the belt of her robe.

"No." He covered her hand. "Let me." He'd done this in his fantasies, but he hadn't imagined the quick tremors that moved along her skin, nor the quick hitch of her breath as he eased the robe off her shoulders. Nor had his imagination quite captured the silky smoothness of her skin. He let out a deep breath. "You're wearing nothing. I wondered." He reined in the urge he had to touch and possess every inch of her.

When his hands moved to the towel at his waist, she closed hers over them. "No. Let *me*."

This time the tremors moved through *him* as his towel slid to the floor and she ran her fingers along the length of his erection.

"I want you."

Sophie wasn't sure who'd said the words. The only reality that she could grasp fully was that he was finally kissing her again. Almost. His lips were nibbling at hers, tasting, as if she were something he wanted to sample slowly. His tongue traced her bottom lip, then brushed at the corner of her mouth. In some part of her mind she questioned how a kiss this soft could set her blood pounding. She wanted it to go on forever.

Moving her hands to his shoulders, she ran her palms along the hard muscles until she could fasten her fingers at the back of his neck. Then she rose to the tips of her toes and tried to get closer. "More."

And then he was kissing her for real, his tongue sliding along hers. The man tasted like a dark, forbidden treat—the wild honey she'd once found in a hive. She hadn't been able to get enough of it. The sweet, addictive flavor had almost been worth the stings she'd suffered later.

She felt his hands move from her shoulders down to her waist. But instead of drawing her closer, they set her away.

"Slow and easy, Princess."

Lifting her gaze to his, she tried to read the expression in his eyes. The blue-green had darkened to the color of an angry sea. It wasn't slow and easy he wanted, and she didn't, either. But the kiss had weakened her again and she couldn't seem to... Then his fingers gripped her waist, turning her so that she could see both of them in the oval mirror next to her bed. The woman she saw reflected there was completely framed by the man. He was dark, dangerous looking. In front of him, she looked pale, almost fragile. The contrast sent a thrill skipping up her spine. Would she ever be able to look in this mirror again without seeing this image?

"I'm going to touch you." His voice was rough and it moved along her skin like sandpaper, igniting little fires as he flattened one large hand against her stomach, drawing her back until her bottom was nestled into his thighs. She could feel his arousal pressing hard against her. Pleasure pierced her as her own body responded, her inner muscles tightening, a dampness gathering between her legs.

"Watch and feel."

She could barely hear his words, her heart was pounding so hard. And her legs…could they really be melting?

His other hand moved to cup her breast. She moaned and her head fell back against his chest. If he weren't holding her, one hand at her breast and the other at her stomach, she would have slipped to the floor.

A horrible thought suddenly occurred to her. Narrowing her eyes, she studied the reflection in the mirror. "I'm not dreaming. Tell me I'm not."

His eyes darkened. "You're not dreaming. Neither am I. Tell me what you want, Princess. This?"

He moved his hand lower over her abdomen, and she began to tremble.

"Lower?"

"Yes."

When his fingers slipped over the curls at the apex of her thighs, she couldn't prevent the moan. "I want…"

She tried to arch up against his fingers, but he held her trapped, pressed tightly against him. Leaning down, he brushed a line of kisses along her throat. "Look at me."

She met his eyes in the mirror.

"I want to see how you feel—how much you want me." He slipped a finger into her and withdrew it.

"Again?" he asked.

"Please."

This time he used two fingers.

The climax began so forcefully and moved through her so fiercely that she cried out as she seemed to splinter apart.

TRACKER LOWERED HER onto the bed, then lay down next to her. The tremors were still moving through her, and his own body was throbbing with the need to take her. Now.

Through sheer force of will, he reined in his desire. No matter how many times he'd fantasized about touching her, pleasuring her, none of it had come anywhere near the reality. He'd never imagined what seeing the pleasure he gave her would do to him.

While she was still steeped in that pleasure, he would love her again. And he would keep it easy and gentle. Raising his hand, he skimmed it down her side, over her hip to her thigh, and began to trace a pattern.

"No," she murmured, opening her eyes. "Stop."

"Stop?" He stilled his hand. "Did I hurt you?"

"Of course not."

"Am I doing something wrong?"

"Oh, no. I didn't mean it that way." She wiggled away from the hand that was resting on her thigh.

"You want me to stop?"

"Good heavens, no. Are you crazy? No one has ever touched me that way. But you haven't...I mean, I haven't..." She managed to lever herself up onto her knees.

When he covered her breast with his hand, she grabbed his wrist. "No, don't. It's my turn to make love to *you*. You just have to give me a second. I think some of my brain cells died.''

She was sure they had. But she wasn't paralyzed, at least. Pressing her hand against his shoulder, she pushed, rolled and wiggled until he was lying beneath her. She might not be as experienced as she would wish, but she'd read *Cosmo*. She knew the value of being on top.

''Princess, let me—''

When he gripped her shoulders, she rose up to straddle his waist. ''Let *me*,'' she teased, looking down at him. ''Haven't you ever heard that turnabout's fair play?''

He studied her for a minute. ''What if I said I'm not finished with my turn yet?''

''That would be good.'' She leaned down, brushed her mouth against his and then withdrew. If she allowed him to deepen the kiss, she would be lost again. And she had plans first. ''How could I argue with that? I just want you to take a little break. I'll be more in the mood for round two if you let me play around a little first.''

His eyes narrowed. ''Play around? What exactly do you have in mind?''

''You don't trust me at all, do you?'' There was wariness mixed with the blatant desire in his eyes, and it filled her with a sense of power and confidence.

''I know when you're up to something, Princess.''

''Me?'' Up to something? Well, if that's what he thought, that's what she would deliver. She'd just have to think ''naughty'' and improvise. Slowly, she trailed a finger from his throat down his chest to a point at the apex of her thighs. The quick hitch of his breath thrilled her. "I might be more trustworthy if I knew your real name. Are you going to tell me or suffer a penalty?"

"What's the penalty?"

Avoiding an answer, she said, "I just want to touch you." She trailed her finger slowly back up to his throat. "You got to touch me." She moved her mouth to his ear. "It only seems fair that I get a turn. And you can even join in after a while. But not until I tell you to." She straightened then and gripped his hands, drawing them over his head. "First, you have to hold on to the bedposts." She was leaning over him, their eyes only inches apart. The wariness was still there, but the heat beneath it nearly singed her skin. Drawing in a deep breath, she said, "Are you game?"

Tracker turned his hands so that he was clasping hers. "Before we start, we have to consider protection."

She found it unbearably sweet that he would think about it. Leaning down, she brushed her mouth against his and whispered, "I'm on the pill. Can we start now?"

In answer, he released her hand and wrapped his fingers around the posts.

The game was on. Sophie was almost giddy with the power of it. And she would have to play it by ear. In bed, she was sure that most of her lovers had found her "nice," but for Tracker she had an almost overwhelming desire to be "naughty." And she would begin in just a moment, but first she had to taste him again. Just for good luck. Leaning down, she brushed her lips against his and slipped her tongue inside. Immediately, she felt the thud of his heart beneath her.

"You taste like toothpaste and..." Pausing, she slipped her tongue in again. "And melted coffee ice cream." She nipped at his bottom lip and then drew it slowly into her mouth. The small sound that he made at the back of his throat seemed to vibrate right through her.

She meant to stop then and ask him what he liked, but already her mouth was moving along the line of his jaw to his ear. He tasted salty and rabidly male. So different. So hot. As she moved her mouth down his throat to his chest, his skin seemed to grow hotter and damper by the moment. She couldn't seem to get enough of it—the smooth outer texture and the iron-hard muscle beneath. When she could go no farther, she levered herself up and shifted so that she was straddling his hips.

Suddenly, she could feel the hardness of his erection beneath her, and she moved instinctively, rubbing herself against it as it pulsed. For her.

She looked at him then. His eyes were half-closed, but she could feel the searing heat of his gaze on her skin, on her breasts. His breathing was ragged, and his knuckles were white where he was gripping the bedposts. When she saw one of them slipping away, she said, "No. My turn isn't over yet."

"Then touch yourself," he ordered in a rough voice. "Touch your breasts."

She hesitated, just barely. She cupped them first, then ran her hands slowly down to her waist. She heard his breathing grow harsher, or was it her own?

She wasn't sure, not with so many little explosions of pleasure whipping through her.

"Lower. Move your hands lower."

But they were already moving until they came to a stop at the juncture of her thighs. Sophie was suddenly aware that she was no longer in control of the game.

"Touch yourself, Princess. Touch yourself for me."

Keeping her gaze fixed on his, she slipped one finger into the slick heat of her femininity. It took all of her strength to say, "It's your turn now. I want you to make love to me, Tracker."

AFTERWARD, Tracker would recall that he felt something snap within him—as clear and as sharp as a rifle shot. But at the moment all he could see was Sophie, and all he could feel was the sharp pain of his need for her—uncontrollable, unreasonable. He had to have her. Now.

Grabbing her by the waist, he rolled her beneath him and thrust into her immediately. She was so tight, so hot. He wanted to go slowly and savor, but he couldn't. Drawing out, he drove himself in harder. Again and again.

She began to move with him then, holding him to her with arms and legs, matching his rhythm as if they were one. As the last shred of his control slipped away, he found the strength to say, "Come with me, Sophie. Come with me now."

And she did, faster and faster, as he drove both of them higher and higher. He felt her close even more tightly around him as the convulsions began to move through her. His climax hit him then, moving through him, carrying him higher and higher until he felt himself shatter.

Sanity returned slowly. He couldn't seem to catch his breath. He couldn't even find the strength at first to move. Then guilt pierced him in one sharp stab and he raised his head to look down at her. He had to have hurt her. He couldn't recall ever taking a woman so violently. There'd been something about the way she'd looked at him when she'd told him to make love to her. He framed her face with his hands. "Sophie, are you all right?"

Her eyes opened then, but it wasn't pain he saw. Her lips curved. "I'm wonderful, except for another batch of dead brain cells. How about you?"

"I didn't hurt you?"

"No. You couldn't."

Reassured somewhat, he levered himself off of her. To his surprise, she immediately rolled over and snuggled next to him, resting her cheek on his chest. The sweetness of the gesture moved through him, pushing away the guilt and fear that remained, and he tightened his arm around her. He had to think. He'd been right the night before. He never should have opened the door to her bedroom. One look at her and his entire plan to protect her had blown up in his face.

Well, it wasn't as though he'd never had to switch to plan B before. The invalid with food poisoning was out and the lover was in. It was hard to regret it, and he was good at improvising. But it was difficult to clear his mind enough to think when she was wrapped around him, clouding his thoughts, filling his senses with her scent, her warmth. The longer he lay there holding her, the harder it was going to be not to roll her on her back and take her again. And again.

A swift surge of panic had him easing away from her. Coffee. Caffeine and a deep gulp of air that wasn't scented with her and he'd be able to think more clearly. He managed to swing his feet off the bed before a hand clamped over his wrist.

"Stop right there. You're not going anywhere."

5

"I'M NOT GOING ANYWHERE," Tracker said.

"You've got that right," she said, keeping a tight grip on his wrist. "You're not going to set foot out of this apartment until we talk."

Tracker frowned. "What makes you think I'd leave?"

"Because that's what you always do. You slip back into those shadows you like so much. And I'm not having it. This is not going to be a one-night stand…or one-morning stand. I don't do them. And I meant to explain that to you before. I think there should be some ground rules."

Tracker struggled to clear his mind. "Okay. You're a little ahead of me here." And that was the problem. She frequently got a little ahead of him. "You want more than a one-night stand."

"I want an affair."

Thoughts tumbled through his mind, and he tried to separate them, evaluate them. As her lover, he could remain close to her twenty-four–seven to protect her. But if they continued as lovers, he might not be able to keep his head clear enough to keep her safe. Bottom line—

"Congress doesn't take this long to pass a bill."

He had to smile. He liked her annoyed almost as much as he liked her pliant and needy and wanting him. "I guess I could be talked into an affair."

"Guess? Talked into?" She released his hand then and gave him one good shove that nearly landed him on the floor. She was about to lunge at him again when he raised his hands, palms out, in surrender.

"Time out. Truce. You were the one who wanted to talk and lay down ground rules, Princess." He had to get out of the bed, away from her scent and her hands. If she lunged at him again, he would take her again. "Why don't you get them all lined up for me while I pour some coffee?" And maybe he could fit in a quick and very cold shower.

Rising, he started toward the door and then stumbled over something lying on the floor. The object slid across the floor and crashed into the wall. "Damn!"

"What?" Sophie asked.

"What indeed?" he asked as he stared down at the items scattered across the floor of the bedroom. Squatting down, he examined them more closely—a long black velvet ribbon, a large stuffed pair of dice and what looked to be a deck of cards. The writing on the dice had the light dawning. Glancing over his shoulder, he saw that Sophie was also staring at the items. The color in her cheeks seemed even higher. "Sex toys?"

"Way to go, Sherlock."

Another surprise. And he had the uncomfortable, fatalistic feeling that there were going to be a lot more. He noted that a faint flush had crept into her cheeks, but her chin had lifted and she was meeting his eyes squarely. Admiration shot through him along with an overpowering urge to tease her just a little more. Glancing down, he picked up the deck of cards and examined a few of them more closely. They were coupons, he discovered. ''This card entitles the bearer to one quickie on demand.'' He might be teasing her, but he could feel himself growing hard. Glancing up, he saw that Sophie was watching him do just that. ''Intriguing. How exactly does it work?''

''You give it to your partner and it entitles her to sex on demand. She gets to name the time and the place.''

Damned if he wasn't tempted to hand it to her. But he needed to think first. And they needed to talk. *Coffee. Cold shower.* Tucking the cards back into the box, he shifted his gaze to the other items. ''You use these much?''

She moistened her lips. ''Not yet. Mac gave them to me last night—a sort of first anniversary present to her maid of honor. She wants me to be as happy as she is.''

With Landry. Jealousy stabbed so quick and deep that for a minute, Tracker couldn't breathe. Mac would have known that Sophie had been dating Landry, and obviously she'd wanted to encourage the match. The guy was perfect for Sophie. Hadn't Tracker said as much to Lucas?

But Sophie had sent the man away last night. Tracker grabbed on to the thought. She wouldn't be using them on Landry. After shoving the cards back into the bag, he picked up the dice.

"These are interesting." He rolled them across the floor. When they hit the nightstand, they rolled back.

"Stroke. Penis."

The questioning look he gave her had her saying, "You have to do whatever it says."

His lips curved. "Oh, I understood that. I'm a trained investigator. I was just wondering who gets to go first, the person rolling the dice or the person watching. You or me, Princess?"

SOPHIE'S MOUTH WENT DRY and then began to water as the image of him stroking himself flooded into her mind. She'd never watched a man do that before, and suddenly she wanted to, almost as much as she wanted to touch him herself.

The fact that his gaze had locked on hers, daring her to answer or make the first move, had the heat pooling deep in her center and a weakness spreading through her limbs. *No*. She immediately stiffened her spine. There was no way he was going to turn her to mush again. Not until they hammered a few things out. "About the affair."

"Want to get started right now?"

She did. Almost as much as she wanted to breathe. "We have to talk first."

He sat down on the floor. "Okay, shoot."

He was enjoying himself, she decided. He'd turned her into a liquid pool of lust, and he was just sitting there, smiling at her, daring her.... And he hadn't even agreed to the affair. The man was so cautious, so suspicious, he could just be stalling until he found a way to leave.

Everyone she'd ever cared about had left her—her parents, and then even Lucas when he'd gone off to school and then the service. She wasn't going to let Tracker get away.

Reaching for the coin on her nightstand, she said, "There's no point in hammering out the details until we decide the main issue. Are we having an affair or not? Why don't we decide it with a toss of the coin?" She held it up between her thumb and forefinger. "Heads, we have a no-strings affair. Tails, you walk out of here and we don't see each other again until Lucas and Mac's next anniversary. Are you game?"

TRACKER DIDN'T SAY anything for a minute. So much for his plan to get some coffee and a cold shower and think. Now his whole game plan was going to be determined on the flip of a coin. Fate. Maybe that was the best way to decide it. He nodded. "Toss it."

She did and held out the coin. "Heads. Now we can hammer out some details."

"Fine. One question. What happens when the affair ends?" Because it would. He had no doubt about that. He and Sophie were too different, and what was burning between them now would surely die down. He would just have to make certain it didn't fade until she was safe and the Puppet Master was behind bars.

"We both walk away—no regrets, no recriminations. And for the length of the affair, we'll be equal partners."

His brows shot up. "Equal partners? Now that has possibilities. As an equal partner, I want to add a couple of things to our deal."

"And they would be?"

"Exclusivity. Neither one of us will see anyone else while we're involved with each other."

"Agreed."

"And let's say we make it a no-holds-barred affair. Are you game, Princess?"

Sophie felt her insides clutch so violently that for a second she thought she was going to have another orgasm. Struggling for control, she ruthlessly cleared her mind and tried to weigh logically what he was offering. Impossible. How could she do that when all she could think of was the challenge of what he was proposing?

"Deal or not, Sophie?"

He was turning her to mush again, and he knew it. Lifting her chin, she said, "No holds barred. Does that mean you'd be willing to use some of those sex toys?"

He grinned at her. "I'm looking forward to it."

Leaning down, she picked up the black velvet ribbon. "How about this? The instructions are on the tag."

He read them and then met her eyes. "I think we could work that in."

No, she was not going to blush. Grace Kelly never had, and Sophie was Mac's role model. Plus, she'd just negotiated a no-strings, no-holds-barred affair, after all. "Then we have a deal."

They extended their hands at the same time. Their palms met in a firm handshake. She was thinking, and she was almost sure that he was, too, of what he'd rolled on the dice—then the phone on her night stand rang.

Not releasing her hand, Tracker reached for it with his free one and held it to her ear.

"Sophie?"

She recognized the voice instantly. Noah Danforth was a graduate student at Georgetown who had worked part-time for her for the past year. She hoped he wasn't calling in sick, because it was going to be a very busy day. "Noah, where are you?" She glanced at the digital clock next to the phone and her eyes widened. She always opened the doors of the shop at ten, and it was fifteen after.

"I'm downstairs in the shop."

"I'm late! I...overslept. I'll be right down."

"Are you all right? I was worried there for a minute when I arrived and you hadn't opened up already."

"I'm fine. Any customers yet?"

"No, but I can see Mrs. Langford-Hughes through the window. She has Chris Chandler and another man with her. They know you're getting that shipment to-day."

"Keep them busy until I get there."

Tracker released her hand at the same moment he replaced the phone.

"I have to go down there."

He smiled at her. "I know." He glanced down at the dice. "I think I can remember where we left off, and we can get back to it tonight." His eyes held amusement and something much more dangerous when they met hers. "You can think about it while you're showering and dressing and putting in a long day in the shop. Anticipation has a heightening effect on pleasure."

The grin he gave her was wicked, promising.

"You can think about it, too." On impulse, she leaned forward and brushed her mouth against his. She was finding it difficult to draw back when a sudden thought had her frowning. "I can't tonight. I have plans."

"A date?" he said, lifting one brow.

"No. It's business. I have to go to a party at Millie Langford-Hughes's house right after work. She's a very important client."

"No problem."

Sophie studied him for a minute and found it impossible to read his expression. He'd agreed to her deal. She should be able to relax now, but she was still worried that he would walk away from her again. That feeling was an old and familiar problem. She'd bared her soul and paid an outrageous sum to a therapist only to "discover" what she already knew too well. She suffered from abandonment syndrome.

And she was still holding Tracker's hand.

"Would you like to come along?"

She thought she saw a flicker of surprise in his eyes.

"Your wish is my command, Princess. And I can give you an extra hand in the shop today if it will help."

"The shop. I have to get down there." Brushing her hair out of her eyes, she slipped from the bed and hurried to the bathroom. At the door, she turned back. "Thanks. Help yourself to coffee, anything."

With a wave, she vanished into the bathroom.

FOR FIVE SECONDS, Tracker debated following her. The Princess had taken control of his head and of another much less controllable part of his body. He was amazed that he'd been able to stop himself from indulging in round two with her—especially when she'd asked if he could manage the little maneuver with the ribbon. His mind filled with the image of having her that way.

In truth, he wanted to have her any way he could, whenever she gave him the chance. His hormones were on a rampage, and that was dangerous. He was going to have to work very hard to keep both his libido and the affair under tight control if he was going to do his job.

His job. Gathering up his clothes, Tracker pulled them on and headed for the kitchen. He didn't believe in lying to himself. Part of the reason he'd agreed to the affair was that he hadn't been able to stop himself. It wouldn't have mattered a bit which way the coin toss had gone.

After tipping coffee into two mugs, he lifted one and took a long swallow. The hot liquid scalded his throat. He could only hope that he hadn't made the biggest mistake of his life. When the truth was out someone was going to get hurt. Sophie, for sure. Just how did he expect her to react when she learned that their affair was an excuse he was using to be her bodyguard for the next few days?

"Ready?"

Tracker glanced up to see her stepping out of the bedroom. He'd seen her in fancier outfits, so there was no reason on earth why the sight of her in red slacks and a brightly flowered silk blouse should hit him so hard. Her hair was twisted up on her head with only a few wisps falling down. And on her feet she was wearing a sexy pair of strappy black sandals. Just looking at her made his mouth water.

"Coffee. You're a lifesaver." Rushing toward the counter, she lifted the mug and took a quick sip, then another before she set the coffee back down. "Not nearly enough, but it will have to do."

Turning, she dashed toward the door. Tracker strode after her, but she was out of sight by the time he reached the hallway. Since he'd installed the security system in Sophie's shop, he was well aware of the layout, but he refamiliarized himself with the place as he followed in her wake. The door at the foot of the stairs led to a small courtyard. Beyond the rose-covered lattices lay an alley that delivery trucks used.

The other door led to the back room of Sophie's shop. By the time he made his way past the packing tables and pushed through the swinging doors, Sophie was already in conference with a young man standing near the cash register. Noah Danforth was a grad student at Georgetown who'd been working part-time for Sophie since she'd opened the shop. He was tall and fair-haired, with narrow, dark-framed glasses and clothes that testified to the fact that he read men's fashion magazines.

Beyond them, three customers studied a blue bowl as if it held the secrets to the universe. The woman was tall, wearing a bright blue suit with a wide-brimmed hat to match. The younger man was short, with a wiry build and long hair he wore pulled back in a ponytail. A diamond flashed on his pinky finger.

The older man had a more portly build and a jovial face with a full beard that had Tracker thinking of both Santa Claus and Ernest Hemingway.

While Sophie moved toward them and was swept up in a round of air-kisses and hugs, Tracker walked over to the man at the cash register and extended his hand. "I'm Tracker McBride, a friend of Sophie's brother. She mentioned that there was a delivery today, and I volunteered to lend a helping hand."

"Noah Danforth," the young man said as he shook Tracker's hand. "She could use the help. One of these days she's going to hurt herself trying to move some of the heavy stuff out of the back room."

"Important customers?" Tracker asked conversationally. He thought he recognized the two men and the woman from Chance's descriptions, but it wouldn't hurt to have his hunch verified.

Noah pitched his voice low. "The woman is Millie Langford-Hughes and the man is Chris Chandler. Currently, he's the designer everyone on Capitol Hill wants to hire, and this is one of his favorite shops."

What Noah didn't add but Chance had told Tracker was that Millie Langford-Hughes was currently the most talked about hostess in the nation's capital, and that she'd pretty much made the reputation of Chris Chandler. Chance had also pointed out that Chandler was in an excellent position to serve as a buyer for the Puppet Master.

"And I believe," Noah continued, "that the bearded man is Sir Winston Hughes, Millie's husband of three months. They've been honeymooning abroad, and this is his first visit to the shop."

Noah's cultured tones, delivered in a murmur, gave Tracker the impression that he was being let in on state secrets. Sir Winston and his new bride were also on Chance's list because Millie was such a frequent visitor to Sophie's shop, Tracker recalled.

In their few minutes of conversation, Tracker decided that Noah Danforth's quiet, controlled style was the perfect foil to Sophie's more outgoing charm.

A bell rang at the front of the shop, and a man in his fifties, with gray hair, a gray suit and tie, entered.

"Excuse me. He's one of our regulars," Noah said in a low tone as he stepped out from behind the cash register. "Congressman Blaisdell, what can I do for you?"

Tracker leaned back against the counter and took a thorough look at the room. It was large and, at first glance, seemed cluttered. But as he let his gaze sweep the room a second time, he saw that there was an artful order to the chaos.

Furniture, cabinets and tables were cleverly arranged to lure people in and facilitate traffic patterns. Vases, paintings and furniture were all displayed with a decorator's touch. Across from him, an armoire in gleaming mahogany stood with its door open, revealing fragile-looking vintage dresses and shawls, their lace yellowed with age. In front of it, a matching dining table, with chairs, was set with crystal, china and silver for eight.

Knowing there were two smaller rooms on the second floor, Tracker wandered toward the stairs.

"This is splendid, simply splendid." Chris Chandler rubbed his hands together in front of the ceramic bowl he'd been studying. "The green-blue tones will fit perfectly in Millie's foyer. How did you ever find it, Sophie?"

"It's from that shop I found on the west coast of England. The owner showcases local artists, and he keeps an eye out for me. I'll place a hold on this bowl for you, but before you make a decision, I'm sure there'll be other pieces in the shipment that's arriving today."

"When?" Millie asked.

Sophie glanced at her watch. "Any minute."

As if on cue, a bell rang at the back of the shop.

"Speak of the devil," Sophie said as she glanced over her shoulder.

"Don't let us keep you, my dear," Millie said. "I just want to be sure that you're coming to my party tonight. I'm introducing Sir Winston to Washington society, and everyone will be there."

"I wouldn't miss it, and I'm bringing a guest."

"Really?"

At Sophie's wave, Tracker joined them and shook hands as Sophie made the introductions.

"I'll see you tonight then," Millie said as Chris and her husband urged her toward the door.

"And I'll be back after lunch to check the shipment. Ta," Chris said.

The moment Sophie disappeared into the back room, Tracker headed toward the stairs and climbed them two at a time to check out the second floor. He'd designed the security system for the store by looking at blueprints, and now he checked out the job his men had done as he wandered through two charmingly decorated bedrooms that were filled to the brim with high-ticket items. A clever thief might get through the first line of defense, but the second layer of the system he'd designed would fool even an expert.

Satisfied that the shop was secure, at least for the time being, he glanced through a narrow glass pane to the courtyard below and watched Sophie take a clipboard from a deliveryman. Then she waved to another man as he popped his head out of the back of the truck.

What Tracker was observing today was that Sophie Wainwright was not just another pretty face. She was also a savvy businesswoman who'd managed in five years to attract many of Washington's movers and shakers into her shop.

That shouldn't surprise him. The first time he'd ever met her, she'd slipped right past him and landed a good right cross to her brother's jaw. She'd taken exception to the fact that Lucas had hired him to spy on her fiancé. And now he was spying on both her and her customers. And he was sleeping with her, too.

Face the facts, McBride. You've wanted to make love to her from the moment you grabbed her away from Lucas that day and she cried in your arms. Looking back, Tracker could see that his attraction to her had started at that first encounter and had led right to where he was today—caught between a rock and a hard place.

He heard the bell jingle in the shop below and then the sound of voices. He didn't take his eyes off Sophie as she climbed up the ramp into the truck.

It wasn't too late to come clean with her. He could

go to her now and tell her what he was really here for. But then he'd have to deal with her reaction. She might tell him to leave. And he couldn't. She'd fooled him completely last summer when she'd switched places with Mac and ended up getting herself kidnapped in Mac's place. She'd almost been killed. This time, Tracker had to make sure that he could protect her.

The two deliverymen began to muscle a crate down the ramp at the same moment that another man walked through the back door of the shop into the courtyard. Tracker recognized John Landry at once. Swearing under his breath, he whirled from the window and headed for the stairs.

If he was going to keep Sophie protected, he'd better keep his mind on the job.

"JUST PUT IT IN the back room," Sophie said. "Noah will uncrate it."

As the two deliverymen slowly eased their burden off the ramp, John Landry stepped into the courtyard.

Sophie waved. "You're just in time to help out."

With a smile, he stepped up to join her in the truck bed. "That's what I came for. What can I do?"

She glanced at her list, and then checked the number on a medium-size crate. Tapping it with her finger, she said, "This is a Louis XIV desk. I have two customers who will drive the price up when they try to outbid each other for it. Think you can manage it alone?"

"I'll give him a hand," Tracker said as he joined

them. "We haven't been introduced. I'm Tracker McBride."

"John Landry."

When neither man extended a hand, Sophie said, "Tracker is a good friend of my brother's, and he's offered his services for the day."

Neither of the men acknowledged that they'd heard her, and for a moment there was silence.

"I'll take this end," Tracker finally said. "You want to grab the other?"

"Fine," Landry said, putting his back into hefting the other end of the crate.

Sophie studied them, frowning a little until they'd managed to get the little desk off the ramp. For a minute there, she thought that one of them might take a swing at the other. But the crate made it without mishap into the shop. With a little shrug, she glanced down at the itemized shipping list, then turned her attention to the numbers on the remaining crates.

Four of them were from the little shop she'd mentioned to Chris and Millie. The owner stocked many items from local artists who produced ceramic pieces, and on her last trip to England Sophie had stopped there twice to place orders.

Finally, she located the crate she was looking for. According to the shipping list, it contained a ceramic horse, and she'd been looking for one for ages.

Lifting the crate, she hurried down the ramp. If she liked it, she would add it to her collection. Feeling triumphant, she raced up the steps to her apartment.

UNLOADING THE TRUCK and arranging the items in the shop took more than two hours. As he helped to uncrate and check pieces for damage, Tracker had ample time to look for drawers with false bottoms or chests with fake backs. But so did Landry, Noah and even Chance, who had joined them for an hour before he opened the gallery. As far as Tracker could see, none of them had found anything.

Then the new stock had to be priced and arranged in the store. As they worked, Tracker had ample opportunity to observe Sophie interacting with the three men. She treated Noah like a younger brother, alternately teasing him, praising him and patting him on the arm.

With Chance she seemed to have the same kind of friendly relationship that she had with Noah. It was only with Landry that she was different. She didn't tease him, nor did she touch him with the same frequency or ease that she did the other two. The first word that came to describe her manner was *reserved*. Oh, there was desire on Landry's part. Tracker had seen it in the man's eyes last night at the party, and in the way he'd been looking at Sophie when he'd joined them in the truck. But in Sophie's manner toward Landry, all Tracker could sense was…regret?

With an effort, he shrugged the thought away. Landry might be part of the smuggling operation. That was what Tracker should be focusing on, not the man's relationship with Sophie.

All of them had worked hard. Even Landry had pulled his weight. But it was Sophie who surprised him the most. Far from assuming the role of princess and ordering everyone around, she was much more likely to try to move the heaviest pieces by herself. Twice he caught her hauling sections of crates out to the alley, and had taken them out of her hands.

When she was finally happy with the arrangement, she'd shooed them into the back room and taken a six-pack of beer out of the small refrigerator she kept there. Setting it on the table, she said, "Enjoy." Then the jingling of the bell had her hurrying out into the shop again.

"I'm going to take a rain check," Chance said, picking up his linen jacket and moving toward the back door. "The gallery calls."

Tracker took one of the bottles Noah was now passing around. "Do you get these shipments often?"

"Two or three times a month," Noah said. "She has two contacts, one in London and a new one along the coast. Business has been good, so she needs a pretty steady supply."

"Are you one of her contacts?" Tracker addressed this question to Landry.

"I've helped her locate a few pieces. I have a wide network of dealers and I'm trying to convince her to use me even more for locating special-order pieces."

Special-order pieces that could be used to smuggle jewels or artwork? Chance might think that Landry was clean, but Tracker wasn't so sure. The man had seemed very interested in each piece that was uncrated.

"She's going to be looking for a Queen Anne desk," Noah said. "Congressman Blaisdell was specifically asking for one this morning."

''Do you know of any other pieces I could keep my eye out for?'' Landry asked.

As the two men continued to talk, Tracker moved to the door to the shop. A young woman had come in, and Sophie was using a step stool to reach something in the window. As he watched, she nearly lost her balance.

''Here, let me.'' In five quick strides he wove his way through the furniture arrangements and gripped her firmly around the waist. ''Which piece?''

''The china doll on the rocking horse.''

The moment he handed it to her, she slipped the price tag off and tucked it into her pocket. Then, stepping down from the stool, she crossed to the woman. ''Here it is.''

The woman turned the doll over in her hands and smoothed the lace collar. ''Melly would love this. I work at the ice-cream store down the block, and every time we walk past your store, she stops to talk to it.''

''It sounds like a perfect match,'' Sophie said. ''How old is Melly?''

''She'll be six on the Fourth of July.'' Then the woman placed the doll on the counter. ''How much is it?''

Sophie picked up the doll and, pursing her lips, examined it. ''The price tag must have fallen off.'' She narrowed her eyes. ''Twenty-five dollars.''

The woman stared at her. ''I thought he said…the young man I talked to said it was over a hundred dollars.'' She reached into her pocket. ''I have the money.''

''You must have talked to Noah, my assistant.''

"Yes. And I'm sure he said—"

Sophie leaned closer to her. "Men. They don't know the first thing about dolls. You ask him about a Louis XIV desk and he can tell you without even looking it up. But he's never accurate about the dolls. The price on this one is twenty-five dollars. Take it or leave it."

The woman opened her mouth and shut it. Tracker could see pride war with her desire to grant her daughter's birthday wish. "I'll take it."

"Good. I'll wrap it for you." Gathering up the doll, Sophie hurried into the back room.

So the Princess was sweet. If he hadn't already liked her, he would have then.

"I'll see you tonight then?" he heard John Landry saying before he reentered the back room.

Tracker frowned. The man just didn't give up. He pushed through the door in time to hear Sophie say, "Of course."

There was no sign of Noah, and Tracker watched John lean down and brush Sophie's cheek with a kiss.

"Why don't I pick you up?" Landry asked.

Tracker took a step into the back room. "Am I interrupting something?"

Sophie shot him a quick look. "John has to leave. But he's going to be at Millie Langford-Hughes's party tonight." She turned back to John. "Tracker is going to be there, too."

"We're going together," Tracker said.

"I see."

See that you do. Though he didn't say the words

aloud, Tracker kept his eyes on Landry until the man exited the shop through the back door.

"You purposely tried to intimidate him," Sophie said.

Tracker shifted his gaze to her and smiled. "I did more than try."

"You did the same thing out in the truck. Why?"

"He wants you and—" Tracker stopped himself before the words slipped out. He was going to say *you're mine*. Instead, he managed a smile. "We have a deal, Princess."

"Yes, we do." She moved toward him then, studying him closely. "And I don't think you're telling me the whole truth. I couldn't help but notice the way you were watching him while we were uncrating the shipment. You were watching everybody. Why?"

She was smart, and if he wasn't careful, the Princess was going to figure out way too much for her own good. Cursing himself, Tracker moved toward her. "It's those damn dice."

"The dice?" Her eyes widened as he caged her against the counter with his arms.

"I don't want you using them with anyone else. Only me." It was the truth, he realized. He was speaking the truth and the worst kind of lie at the same time. But he couldn't let her suspect his real reason for being in her shop and in her bed. Years of living on the streets had made him skillful at lying convincingly.

"You're jealous?"

"Seems so. He's nice, and I'm not." Tracker moved closer and watched her eyes darken around the image of himself that he could see in them. No, he wasn't nice. He would use any means to keep her safe. Including sex. Lowering his head, he brushed his mouth along her jaw to her ear. Then he whispered softly, "Do you remember what the dice said, Princess?"

"Yes." Her voice was breathless. Her scent was filling him.

"Tell me."

"No."

"No?" Surprised, he drew back slightly until his eyes met hers. There was desire there and mischief, too.

"Why don't I show you?" she said instead.

Her hand was on him then, moving along the entire hard length of his erection. Tracker had to struggle to swallow a moan. "Sophie."

"I want to do this without your clothes in the way. And I want to keep touching you like this until you come."

He gripped the edge of the counter behind her, hard. He could imagine all too well how it would feel to have her hands on him without the barrier of clothes. Right now, she wouldn't have to work very hard to get her wish. He wouldn't have to work very hard to get his, either—he could picture slipping her out of her red slacks, lifting her to the counter and burying himself deep inside of her. For a moment he allowed the images to play themselves out in his mind. Then he said in a soft voice, "In another minute, Melly's mom might be very shocked."

Slowly Sophie drew her hand away. Then she met his eyes. "We'll finish this later."

"Your wish is my command, Princess." Tracker released his grip on the counter and eased himself out of her way. As he watched her pick up the package and walk off, he drew in a deep breath and let it out.

When she reached the door, she turned back. "And then it will be my turn to roll the dice."

Lust and nerves settled into a hard knot in his center. Using sex to distract Sophie was turning into a double-edged sword.

THE PUPPET MASTER was smiling at his companion as he punched numbers into the speakerphone. The chess game was going well. And within a very short time, he would have the last coin.

As soon as someone lifted the receiver on the other end, he said, "Report."

"I don't have it."

His smile faded. "You've failed me?"

"No. I swear to you it's not in the shop."

With one hand he swept the chess pieces off of the board in front of him. "It was shipped. I have a copy of the shipping list in front of me. You have failed me."

"No. I'll get ahold of it. I have an idea of what might have happened."

"What *might* have happened?"

"You'll have it soon. I'll deliver it in person."

"You have until midnight."

He cut the connection and summoned a smile for his companion. "My apologies. We'll have to start a new game."

6

THEY WERE LATE. Ordinarily, Sophie would have been annoyed with herself. She was always punctual, always prepared when it came to business, and a cocktail party at Millie Langford-Hughes's house was simply an extension of her workday. But Sophie was finding it very difficult to work up any regrets about her tardiness when it had been caused by the insatiable lust of the man sitting next to her.

She shot Tracker a quick sideways glance. He was staring straight ahead and wearing sunglasses against the glare of the early evening sun. It was impossible to tell what he was thinking.

She hoped he was thinking about what had happened in her shower after he'd joined her there. He hadn't wanted to. He'd told her that much as he'd lifted her and pressed her against the wall. He'd told her again when she'd wrapped her legs around him and he'd entered her. But he couldn't stop himself. And he hadn't been gentle. A smile curved her lips. She hadn't wanted him to be. The roughness of his lovemaking, the desperation that she'd felt in his hands, in each thrust of his body… Just thinking about it sent an arrow of pleasure shooting through her. The

idea that a man could want her that much had filled
her with such a sense of power.

The gentleness had come afterward when he'd held
her in his arms until the water had turned cold. It
would be so tempting to interpret that gentleness as
meaning that he cared for her. But she couldn't let
herself expect that. She wouldn't. People disappointed
you when you did.

Seeing the yellow light ahead, she pressed her foot
on the brake and took the corner on two wheels.

Tracker slammed a hand into the dashboard. "Easy,
Princess."

Sophie glanced over at him. He seemed even larger
in the front seat of her Miata. The thought struck her
then that they were racing through the streets in a convertible with the top down just as Grace Kelly and
Cary Grant had in *To Catch a Thief.* Only Grace
hadn't just come from a bout of hot sex in the shower.
Sophie laughed as she slammed on the brakes at a red
light.

"Want to share the joke?" Tracker asked.

She turned to him then, and her heart did a little
somersault in her chest. He was dressed in black—not
the jeans and T-shirt that he'd worn in the shop all
day, but in slacks and an elegant silk shirt, open at the
throat. Just looking at the few curls of chest hair that
were visible had her throat going dry. The sunglasses
kept her from seeing his eyes, and made him seem
even more dangerous.

A funny little ache began to grow deep inside of
her. How could she want him again so soon? "I was
just thinking that I'd like to blow everything off and

just keep driving—maybe up into the mountains some-where. Have you ever been tempted to do something like that?'' she asked.

"Just about every day in my misspent youth."

"It's hard to believe you had one. You seem so dedicated to your work."

"I think this is a case of the pot calling the kettle black. I've seldom seen anyone as dedicated as you."

The pleasure that his words brought moved through her. But she wasn't going to be distracted. "Did you ever give in to the temptation?"

"Too many times to count." Reaching over, he tucked a wisp of hair behind her ear. "If you wanted to blow the party, I'll bet you could find a way to persuade me."

Several methods slipped into Sophie's mind and she was very tempted to try them one at a time, but a sharp honk from the car behind her had her gripping the wheel and making a sharp turn. Gathering her thoughts, she said, "Millie would never forgive me." She flicked him a look as she turned into a circular drive. "Although the persuading part sounds interest-ing. How about a rain check?"

He grinned at her. "You got it. I'll even play hard to get."

She was laughing as she handed the key to the valet who opened her car door. When she joined Tracker on the other side, she pitched her voice low. "You weren't playing very hard to get in the shower."

His expression sobered. "I wasn't easy on you."

Sophie studied him for a minute. No, he wasn't a

man who would ever be easy on a woman. Then she smiled slowly. "I guess I'll just have to get even."

He studied her. He'd been rough with her in the shower. But he hadn't hurt her, and he was beginning to believe that he wouldn't—at least not physically. Finally, he said, "This party can be your revenge."

"You don't like parties?" she asked as he took her arm and led her up the steps to the house.

"I can think of several other things I'd rather be doing," he said as a man who looked more like a linebacker than a butler opened the door.

"Good evening, Miss Wainwright."

"Good evening to you, too, Callahan." Standing on tiptoes, she brushed a kiss against his cheek. "This is my brother's friend, Tracker McBride. Ms. Langford-Hughes knows that I'm bringing him."

Callahan gave Tracker an assessing look, then nodded. "They're in the solarium."

"I didn't know they used bouncers at elite Washington parties," Tracker said as they moved down a wide hall that bisected the two wings of the house.

"Don't worry. Callahan has been with Millie's family forever. He's really a sweetheart. Sir Winston is her third husband, and I think part of Callahan's job is to bounce the husbands once they turn out to be cads."

"Is Sir Winston likely to turn out to be a cad?"

Sophie shook her head with a smile. "Not that I can tell. He was very attentive to her at the shop, and Millie claims this is her first love match."

The solarium was a huge room that boasted a glass ceiling, a variety of potted plants and trees, and French doors that opened onto a flagstone patio and the gardens. The air was filled with the scents of food and flowers. Tables laden with delicacies lined one wall, and a string quartet was situated at the other side of the room. Mozart blended with the sounds of laughter and glasses clinking as the bigwigs of the nation's capital sipped drinks and made deals. Sophie straightened her shoulders and scanned the crowd eagerly.

"You really enjoy this kind of thing, don't you?" Tracker asked.

"Each one of those people is a potential customer. I look at them and I hear my cash register going *cha-ching, cha-ching.*"

"You remind me of your brother."

Surprised, she looked at him then. "I'm not like Lucas at all. He's the dutiful son who took over the company and saved it. During the two years I worked there, I could never please him. He always wanted to be so conservative, and I wanted to try new things. I started my own business because I had to get away from that."

"You needed the freedom of being your own boss. But you have the same determination Lucas has to make the business a success, and your shop means as much to you as Wainwright means to Lucas."

She frowned as she turned back to scan the crowd again. "Okay. You're right about my wanting freedom. And I can see some similarity in terms of our dedication to our work, but in other ways Lucas and I are as different as…well, you and I—" She grabbed his hand. "Millie and Chris Chandler are on their way toward us." She took a step forward, then glanced back at him. "You're going to be incredibly bored, aren't you?"

"I'll manage. You go ahead and do your thing."

Drawing in a deep breath, she slipped her hand into her pocket and pulled out a card. She'd brought it with her, and she was going to use it. "I want you to be thinking about this."

As he took it and read it, Sophie held her breath while her heart jittered. She'd slipped the "quickie on demand" card from the deck while she'd been dressing, but she hadn't intended to give it to Tracker until they were leaving. "In terms of anticipation, I thought it might relieve the boredom of the party for you."

He still didn't say anything, but when his eyes finally met hers, she felt the heat streak right down to her toes. "I'm going to do more than think about this, Princess."

The paralyzing look was back in his eyes, and Sophie thought of her red convertible and how easy it would be to grab Tracker's hand and make a run for it. The hills of Monte Carlo were beckoning.

"Sophie, my dear, you're never late. I was worried." Millie Langford-Hughes took her hands and kissed the air on both sides of Sophie's face.

Then Sophie found her hands grasped in Sir Winston's large ones. "I'm so glad you could come, my dear. It means a great deal to Millie and, therefore, to me."

For a second, as she glanced into his twinkling gray eyes, Sophie felt a tug of familiarity, just as she had in her shop. There was such warmth, such sincerity in his eyes. She couldn't figure out if he reminded her of

Santa Claus or Ernest Hemingway. Either way, there wasn't a doubt in her mind that this time Millie had indeed found her love match.

"Nice to see you again, Mr. McBride," Millie said, taking his hand. "I'm so happy you could come, and I have someone who is just dying to meet you."

Tracker gave Sophie one last look before Millie pulled him away in the direction of the patio. Sir Winston gave them a wave and then followed in his wife's wake.

"Oh, my," Chris said in a voice meant only for Sophie's ears. "I saw the way McBride was looking at you." He paused to fan himself. "If we could bottle that, we wouldn't have to worry about energy conservation. I'd say he's a bit more to you than your brother's friend."

Sophie turned to him and prayed that she wasn't blushing. "He's my friend, too."

"Sure he is," Chris said, taking her arm and tucking it through his. "And I won't breathe a word of it to a soul. He's much more your type than the buttoned-down egocentric banker type you almost married last year."

Sophie choked on a laugh. Chris's description fit her ex-fiancé to a T.

"As for that Landry fellow, he might as well be a clone of your ex. You're much better suited to Mr. McBride."

"Better suited?" Sophie turned to study him, no mean feat while Chris was dragging her through the crowd. "Why would you say that? Tracker and I don't have anything in common."

Chris waved a hand and shot her a sly wink. "You have passion. It virtually crackles in the air around you, and that's not a bad place to start. But enough talk about your love life. Before I introduce you to this prospective client I have all lined up for you, I want to know when your next shipment is coming in. I have another client who is interested in picking up some of the ceramic work by the same artist who made that lovely blue-green bowl you tagged for Millie. He's looking for something with an equestrian theme." Chris leaned close again. "I think he has some kind of fetish for horses."

Sophie crossed her fingers behind her back. "I'll certainly keep an eye out for that."

MILLIE CUT A WIDE SWATH though the crowd, shooting like an arrow toward a couple on the far side of the room.

"I want you to meet my niece, Meryl Beacham," Millie said to Tracker. "She runs the art gallery next to Sophie's shop." She pulled up short in front of a striking woman with black hair in a straight, angular cut. Chance was standing next to her.

"Meryl, I want you to meet Tracker McBride, a friend of Lucas and Sophie Wainwright. And this is Carter Mitchell, Meryl's gallery manager."

"Carter." Tracker took the hand that Chance offered, then turned his attention to Meryl. "It's a pleasure."

"A mutual one," Meryl said in a throaty voice.

"I knew you two would hit it off. Enjoy," Millie

said with a wave of her hand as she took Sir Winston's arm and swept him away.

Meryl shifted her gaze to the archway of the solarium. "My aunt is a huge busybody, and she introduces every male to me that she can find. However, I think we're safe now. A four-star general has just appeared on her radar screen. Aunt Millie has bigger fish to fry, for a while anyway." Then she turned her attention back to Tracker. "Why haven't I seen you around Sophie's shop before?"

"I'm on vacation here." The brunette had an easy, open manner, but the fact that Chance hadn't mentioned that he and Tracker had "met" earlier in Sophie's shop warned him to be careful. "I've been visiting out at Lucas's estate in Virginia." That much was true. Any number of people who had attended the party could attest to the fact that he'd been there.

"So Sophie discovered you first and you're taken?"

Tracker smiled then, finding her frankness disarming. "You might say that."

"Just my luck." She glanced at Chance. "I'm standing here with the two best-looking men in the room. One of them's gay and the other is already spoken for. C'mon, Carter, if I can't play with Mr. McBride here, I'd better put you to work marketing my gallery to all these potential customers."

Tracker turned to study the room, his gaze going immediately to Sophie. She was talking to a tall man with a waxed mustache—Charles Lipscomb, England's newly appointed ambassador to the United States. She'd spoken the truth when she'd said that she was here to work. When Tracker considered the day she'd already put in, his admiration for her went up another notch. He'd always thought of her as a pampered, rebellious princess. But he'd never in his wildest dreams imagined that she felt herself to be a misfit in her own family. He could empathize with the feeling. In the string of foster homes he'd been shuffled to, he'd never once fit in.

Shifting his gaze, he glanced toward the archway that all new arrivals had to pass through, and spotted John Landry. Well, except for Noah Danforth, that completed the list of suspects that Chance had originally given him. And Tracker still didn't have a clue as to who was putting Sophie's life in danger.

"Sometimes this job sucks," Chance said at his elbow. "My lovely companion and boss allows me a five-minute break to smoke. Me and this Scotch are heading out to the patio. See you there in a minute?"

Tracker waited until Chance had made his exit before he pushed himself away from the wall and wandered through the French doors. He spotted Chance on the other side of some potted trees and joined him. "Your boss is an interesting woman."

Chance grinned at him. "If it weren't for my cover, that lady and I could be having a very good time." He took a drag of his cigarette.

"You know what they say," Tracker said. "It's best not to mix business with pleasure."

Chance's brows shot up as he blew out smoke. "And here I always thought you were a man who walked what you talked."

Tracker frowned as he glanced back at the French doors. "This is different. Sophie's different. And it's complicated.'' He spotted Landry making his way to the side of the room Sophie was on. "Right now I don't know of any other way to stay close enough to protect her.''

"It sounds like great work if you can get it.'' Chance lifted his glass to Tracker.

Tracker pinned the other man with a cool look. "I didn't plan it this way, but I'll do whatever is necessary to protect her. It's tricky, because she's every bit as smart as her brother.''

Chance gave a low whistle.

Tracker met his eyes. "Yeah. That smart. We've got to nail this guy fast. Sophie is going to figure out what I'm up to, and once she does, I can't predict what she'll do except order me out of her life. I want to know everything that you know.''

"I've told you—''

"Cut the shit. Tell me why you can't let your boss know that you were in Sophie's shop helping to unload that shipment. She wasn't on the list of suspects you gave me.''

With an easy smile that didn't reach his eyes, Chance tossed his cigarette to the flagstones and ground it beneath his foot. "Relax. I don't want Meryl to know how friendly I've become with Sophie. It's partly to protect my cover. She's a bit jealous of Sophie's success. Both of them come from the same background. However, Meryl just dabbles in commerce, while Sophie has a real talent for it.'' Chance offered his drink to Tracker. "Peace offering. I figure I have five minutes before Meryl crooks her little finger at me and I have to go back to work.''

Tracker took a swallow of Scotch and passed the glass back. "Talk fast."

"What I told you at Lucas's party is correct as far as it goes. We don't know who's behind the smuggling. What we do know is the Puppet Master has connections that go very high up on both sides of the Atlantic." Chance took a long swallow of his Scotch. "It's no accident that I'm working in Meryl's shop. She and her aunt Millie are very well connected. Either of them could easily be the middleman, or they could be pawns, just as Sophie is a pawn. We just don't know."

"You got any good news?"

Chance met his eyes steadily. "No. We're dealing with a very dangerous individual. The best thing that you can do is to stick to Sophie like glue and give the impression of business as usual."

Tracker nodded. "Okay, let's try another angle. Do you have any idea which piece today held the coin?"

"No. I couldn't locate it. But I'm working on it. I should have an answer before I leave the party tonight."

"Carter, I need you."

The two men turned to see Meryl Beacham standing at the French doors.

Chance moved toward her. "Coming, darling."

Biting back his impatience, Tracker followed them back into the solarium. He had no choice but to watch and wait.

EACH TIME SHE HAD a chance, Sophie found her gaze seeking out Tracker. Currently, he was surrounded by women. No surprise there. She recognized the tall, leggy blonde as being the president's press secretary. Another one was clerking for the chief justice of the Supreme Court. What surprised her was the way Tracker fit in as if he'd been navigating his way through the Washington social scene all his life.

For a man who didn't enjoy parties, he certainly didn't look like this one was bothering him any. For the first time since she'd met him, Sophie wondered what he did when he wasn't being Lucas's head of security.

"You're looking lovely in that dress."

Sophie turned to find John Landry at her side, offering her a glass of white wine. She took it gratefully. "Thanks. You're looking very well yourself." And he was. He was the kind of man she'd always thought she'd fall in love with. The kind of man she'd done her best to fall in love with three times.

Sophie frowned as she took a swallow of her wine. Now, where had that thought come from? And why hadn't she ever realized before that Bradley, Sunny and John were all the same type—solid, good-looking businessmen and just the kind of person a Wainwright should marry?

She shifted her gaze to Tracker. All of the men she'd pictured getting serious about were the complete opposite of Tracker McBride. Tracker was the kind of man you kidnapped in your red convertible and thought of racing away into the mountains with. Or had hot sex in your shower with. And she'd always wanted someone she could depend on, someone who would be there and never walk away.

"Penny for your thoughts," John said.

"They're not worth even that." She was not getting serious about Tracker McBride. That was not part of the deal. They were simply having a no-strings, no-holds-barred affair between equal partners. Those were the rules they'd both agreed to, and Sophie believed in honoring her agreements. At the end of it, they would both walk away. Ignoring the little band of pain that settled around her heart, she managed a smile as she turned to John Landry.

"I'm just zoning out a little. It's been a long day. You have my permission to pinch me if I do it again."

"You should get more help in that shop."

Sophie studied him for a moment. There was something different about him tonight—a hint of nerves or excitement beneath his usual smooth exterior. "Something's bothering you."

"You're very perceptive. Something has been bothering me all evening but it's finally clicked."

"What?" she asked.

"Nothing important. I met someone tonight—a stranger, but he seemed familiar. And I just remembered where I saw him before. However, what I really came over here to tell you was that I talked with Matt Draper today."

Sophie smiled. "I wish he was here tonight. He'd be the man of the hour. You have no idea how many people are suddenly interested in the ceramic pieces I've been ordering through his shop. I'm going to have to call him."

Landry took a sip of his wine. "He mentioned the shipment you received today when he was talking to me. He wondered how you liked the ceramic horse he sent."

Sophie smiled. "You can tell him that I liked the horse so much that I took it right upstairs to unpack. No, on second thought, I'll tell him myself. I'm calling him tomorrow to tell him I need more where that came from."

"I'll mention it to him when I see him." Landry glanced at his watch. "I'll be flying back to England tomorrow and I have some loose ends to tie up."

Sophie stared at him. "I thought you planned to stay for another few weeks."

Landry glanced to where Tracker was standing, then met her eyes. "I'd hoped to, but my plans have changed, and so, it seems, have yours. I'm sorry for that, Sophie. I'd hoped…" Leaning over, he brushed her lips with his. "I'll give you a call next time I'm in D.C. to see if anything has changed."

TRACKER HAD NEVER FELT his blood move to the boil quite so quickly. Only years of working to restrain his temper allowed him to stay right where he was, talking to a tall woman who was boring him senseless, while he watched every move that Landry made. The kiss was the final straw. It reminded him of what was reality. Sophie and he came from different worlds. She belonged with the people in this room. He didn't.

And as Landry walked away, she looked as if she'd lost something. That was what had brought his blood to the boil. Jealousy, anger, frustration. Hell, they were bad enough when they weren't mixed with the fear that he wasn't going to be able to keep her safe. And there was something else, too. He wanted to take that sad look off of her face.

"Damn it," he muttered.

"What did you say?"

With an effort, he turned his attention to the tall blonde who was the president's press secretary, and smiled. "I beg your pardon. I just remembered a phone call I forgot to make."

EVEN THOUGH HER BACK WAS toward him, Sophie knew the minute Tracker started toward her from the far side of the room. It occurred to her that the special awareness that she always felt when he was around had only grown since they'd made love. Even Chris Chandler had seemed to be aware of it. She felt more alive, as if her life had gone from black and white to color, and she couldn't recall ever feeling quite so free. She wanted it to last.

As he drew closer, she turned and her gaze dropped to his mouth. It took only that to trigger a memory of what his lips felt like on hers. And she wanted to feel them again, on her breasts and on that most intimate part of her. The center of her body heated and then pooled into liquid.

When he reached her and his hand closed over hers, it felt like a brand. "I want you to come with me."

"I can't leave the party yet," she managed to answer.

His gaze never left hers as he slipped a card out of his pocket and gave it to her. "I'm not asking you to."

She glanced down at the card, recognizing it as the "quickie on demand" coupon she'd given him earlier.

"Here?" She nearly gulped.

"And now. Those are the rules of the game as you explained them to me, right?"

She took a quick look at the people around them. No one seemed to be listening in on their conversation, thank heavens. "We can't."

He flashed her a wicked grin. "Yes, we can. C'mon."

"Tracker, I—"

"No holds barred. Remember?"

She bit back whatever else she might have said when she realized that she was already moving through the crowd with him toward the far end of the solarium.

"Are you having second thoughts about our deal, Princess?" he asked as he turned down a hallway and opened the first door.

It was a powder room. He urged her into it, and with the door shut, the words *close quarters* took on new meaning. There was barely room for one person between the small toilet and the sink. His hands were on her waist, turning her around so that their bodies were just touching.

"I'm collecting on that coupon, Princess. Unless you want to back out?"

Her chin shot up. "I don't back out of agreements."

He nodded, stepping back against the door. "Then take off your panties."

7

A THRILL WENT THROUGH HER as she reached down and grasped the thin silk of her dress. Out of the corner of her eye, she could see her reflection in the long mirror that covered the narrow wall above the vanity. But it was more interesting to watch Tracker. His eyes had narrowed and focused on the hem of her dress as she inched it up her thighs. She could actually see the muscles in his jaw tighten when she finally had the dress up to her waist. Her own breath was backing up in her throat as she slipped her thumbs under the elastic of her panties.

''The operative word here is *quickie*.'' His voice sounded strained.

''Really? Am I doing something wrong?'' From the look in his eyes and the tension she could see in his body, she was doing something right. The power of his reaction held an excitement all its own. Slowly, she began to push the elastic inch by inch over her hips and down her thighs. The pulse at Tracker's throat had begun to beat, and she felt her own blood quicken in response.

He waited only until she'd stepped out of the panties before he moved toward her. Slipping his hands beneath the hem of her dress, he pushed it up and cupped her hips in one smooth movement. By the time he lifted her and braced her against the wall, she had her legs wrapped around him, doing everything she could to urge him closer.

"Quiet," he whispered in her ear.

The urgency in his voice stilled her at once. Then she heard it, the quick click of high heels on parquet floors. Sophie was sure that neither one of them drew a breath as the sound of the footsteps grew closer and then gradually faded away.

He drew back then. His voice was strained, his gaze steady on hers when he said, "Do you want to stop?"

"No. I…what I'd like to do is try that black velvet ribbon."

Tracker's eyes widened.

She'd shocked him, and the realization thrilled her. "You said you could do it…."

"You want to play that game *here?*"

"No holds barred." She thought her heart might pound right out of her chest as he lowered her to the floor. But she wasn't going to back out now. The sight of him unbuckling his belt and unzipping his slacks had her fumbling as she took the ribbon out of her purse. She wasn't even sure why she'd brought it. She couldn't possibly have foreseen that she would actually suggest using it at Mrs. Langford-Hughes's party.

When Tracker lowered his briefs, her throat went dry and her free hand moved of its own accord to touch him.

He took her wrist firmly in his and spoke softly. "We'll play the dice game later, Princess. Someone could come along at any minute."

Then, lifting her hand, he pressed his lips to it. "We'll take it slow and easy…at first. And any time you want to stop, you'll let me know?"

Stop? In another moment she was going to die if he didn't *start*.

Then he lowered himself to the toilet seat and pulled her astride him. "Relax."

She couldn't. He was shifting her on his lap, and she could feel his erection pressing against her, heavy, hot, seeking. But it wasn't close enough. Even as she tried to wiggle closer he slid a finger into her, then slowly drew it out.

The streak of pleasure was so sharp she nearly cried out. But it wasn't enough.

"Shh." His voice was a breath in her ear. "We can't make any noise." His hands gripped her waist and he lifted her. Finally, his erection probed her just a little. Just enough to have the ache within her growing.

"Don't tease me, she said in a tight whisper. "Please."

"Lean forward a little and brace your hands on the sink."

She did as he asked, and she felt him press into her a little more. The ribbon. She was supposed to do something with it. Struggling, she tried to picture the diagram as she leaned forward. She had to loop it around him.

"Wait."

He stilled immediately, and she nearly cried out in protest.

"Do you want me to stop?" he asked.

"No. I just can't remember what to do with the ribbon. I need to think for a minute."

"Look in the mirror, Princess."

All thought of the ribbon faded when she saw the image reflected there. He was sitting behind her, his face tight and strained, his eyes so hot she was sure that they alone were causing the flames that were searing through her. And she didn't even recognize the woman. She looked sexy and wanton. And hungry.

"I've been fantasizing about taking you this way ever since you showed me that ribbon and asked me to read the instructions."

His words had her insides clenching, but it wasn't enough. She needed more of him now. "But the ribbon…"

"Who needs it?" He moved his mouth down her neck and along her shoulder. The fact that she could see him in the mirror as well as feel the heat of his lips and tongue was making her so hot that she thought she might just turn into steam.

"I'm going to take you now."

She felt his teeth sink into her shoulder, and suddenly he was stretching her, filling her, deeper than he'd been before. The angle and the sensation were so different. She had one moment to absorb the incredible feeling before he withdrew and entered her again.

When she tried to move against him, he held her still.

"We're going to take this slow and easy, Princess. I don't want to hurt you."

"You won't." She didn't care if he did. She just

wanted him to move, to ease the incredible pressure that had begun to build inside of her.

At last he did, keeping the thrusts slow at first. With each one, he seemed to fill her even more deeply, and each time he began to withdraw, she tightened around him, gripping him as hard as she could to keep him inside of her.

All the time she could see the little contest going on between them in the mirror—their bodies moving, mating, straining to become one. But it was never quite enough. She needed more. And just when she thought she might die from the wanting, he moved his hand down from her waist to just the right spot between her legs and began to thrust harder and faster.

She felt her climax begin, one incredible wave washing through her, around her. Before she let it take her completely, she reached behind her to grip his arm and whispered, "Come with me, Tracker. Right now."

She felt him thrust, and even as the world spun away, he shuddered against her.

AT FIRST TRACKER THOUGHT the sound was his heart pounding. But it stopped suddenly, and a woman's voice said, "Is anybody in there?"

How long had she been knocking? Gathering his thoughts, he was stunned to realize that he was cradling Sophie on his lap with no clear idea of how she'd gotten there or how long he'd been holding her. He was still shuddering, still struggling to breathe. His body still wasn't taking orders from his brain.

From the moment he'd told her to take off her panties, the need had begun to build in him until it had become a searing pain. No woman had ever made him hurt before. His last rational thought had been to offer to stop, and then she'd mentioned that damn black ribbon. That reckless look in her eye, the thought of taking her that way, had completely short-circuited his brain.

Now her head was resting on his shoulder, and she was holding him as if she never wanted to let him go. The power that she wielded over him was so great that he didn't want to let her go, either.

The knock sounded again on the door.

Tracker drew in a deep breath. "I'll just be another minute."

Sophie lifted her head just enough to whisper into his ear, "We're both caught with our pants down."

He felt the laugh beginning to build, and ruthlessly controlled it. When he drew back far enough so that she could meet his eyes, hers were bright with amusement. Another woman would have been embarrassed or even angry. Sophie never ceased to amaze him.

She mouthed the words, *"What are we going to do?"*

He leaned closer and nipped the lobe of her ear. "Want to go for seconds?" Then he quickly smothered her laugh by covering her mouth with his. One taste was all it took to have need building again. Incredible. Would it always be this way? Breaking off the kiss, Tracker met her eyes again. She looked as surprised and as ready as he was.

"We'd better both get our pants back on," he whispered as he eased her off his lap. Then he reached to pull his own up. When he bent down to retrieve hers, he saw the coupon that they'd exchanged. He handed it to her with the panties. "Your turn."

With a grin, she tucked it into the top of her dress, then reached down to tug up the hem.

Shoving down a groan, Tracker stilled her hands. "That's what got us into this compromising position," he breathed.

"You're not suggesting I go out there without my panties?"

"As enticing as that sounds, I just want you to wait until I'm on the other side of that door."

For the first time, Sophie frowned. "But I can't stay here. That woman—"

Tracker squeezed her hand and winked. "Leave it to me, Princess."

Placing his hands on her shoulders, he turned them both in a circle until they had reversed positions, and then he nudged her into the corner between the toilet and the door. "The moment I close the door, turn the lock."

Sophie did exactly as he asked.

"Sorry about that." The muffled sound of Tracker's voice carried through the door. "Nobody warned me about the seafood in the canapés."

"No problem." The woman's voice was a deep, throaty purr. It carried none of the impatience that had been evident earlier. "Are you going to be all right?"

"Good as new."

Sophie saw the handle turn and heard the door click against the jamb.

"It's locked," the woman said. The handle turned again.

"Here, let me." The handle turned a third time. This time the door hit the jamb with a solid clunk.

"You're absolutely right."

The surprise in Tracker's voice had Sophie clamping a hand over her mouth.

"What am I supposed to do now?" the woman asked.

"Not to worry. You know, in a house this size, there must be other powder rooms. I'll help you find one."

As the footsteps faded down the parquet floors, Sophie wiggled out of the corner Tracker had tucked her into. She owed him one. Glancing down at the panties and the black ribbon she still held in her hand, she finally let out the giggle she'd been holding in. She owed him more than one, and she was going to collect. Now that she knew the position in the diagram was not only anatomically possible, but incredible, she was going to have to work on her technique with the ribbon. Tucking it in her purse, she studied herself in the mirror.

She wasn't the same woman she'd been twenty-four hours ago. She'd never in her life sneaked into a bathroom with a man to have sex. And until today, she never would have imagined that Tracker McBride would ever do anything like that either. He was different from the man who'd haunted her dreams for the past year. He was an even better lover than she'd imagined—and he was fun! She'd just never expected the man who'd annoyed her so much to bring such bright explosions of pleasure into her life.

Wiggling into her panties, Sophie continued to study her own reflection in the mirror. Thanks to

Tracker, she was discovering things about herself she'd never known. Oh, she'd always enjoyed sex. But she'd never before wanted it with the intensity that she felt with Tracker. She'd never wanted to taunt and tease a man the way she did him. Nor had she ever thought of herself as an exhibitionist, but it had thrilled her to take off her panties and watch his response. Just thinking about it had desire curling inside of her again.

With it came a little sliver of worry. How was she going to let Tracker go when the affair was over?

HE'D NEVER SEEN a woman work harder, Tracker decided a little over an hour later. Since she'd emerged from the bathroom, Sophie had managed to work the entire solarium. He was beginning to understand that her shop meant as much to her as his job did to him. And he'd come very close to blowing his.

What in hell had he been thinking when he'd given her that coupon and taken her to the powder room? No, the real question was what had he been thinking with? Certainly not with his head. If they'd been discovered, it could have damaged a business reputation that she'd worked very hard to build. And he'd been negligent to leave her there alone while he'd run interference with the large, buxom lady who'd knocked so adamantly on the door.

Tracker let his glance shift back to Sophie. She was standing half a football field away. And there was far more than space separating them. He'd do well to remember that his job was to protect her, and he'd better keep his mind on doing just that.

He was frowning when his cell phone rang. He

moved quickly toward the doors that opened onto the patio. No one had his cell phone number except Lucas and the men who worked security at the Wainwright office complex. His security team only called him in an emergency.

Flipping the phone open, he said, "Tracker."

"We got a call from the D.C. police, boss. A Detective Ramsey says there's been a break-in at Sophie Wainwright's shop, but the alarm didn't go off."

"When?" Tracker asked as his mind raced.

"He wouldn't give any details. He just said that it's very important that Ms. Wainwright call him."

A tight ball of fear settled in Tracker's stomach. Lucas and Mac had had some dealings with Detective Ramsey last year, and Tracker had checked the guy out. According to the information he'd dug up, Ramsey worked in a special unit for the DCPD. It specialized in high-profile disappearances and homicide.

"I want you to call Ramsey back and tell him that Ms. Wainwright is on her way to the shop."

"Will do."

Slipping his cell phone back into his pocket, Tracker headed toward her. He wasn't going to let Sophie talk to Ramsey unless he was right there at her side.

A BREAK-IN. Sophie was still trying to get her mind around it when Tracker pulled the car into the garage in the alley behind her shop. As far as she knew there hadn't been a break-in anywhere on Prospect Street since she'd been in business. The alarm system had been installed and updated by Wainwright Enterprises' security people. She glanced at Tracker as they left the garage and headed toward the courtyard. His expression was serious, but he was holding her hand. That one simple gesture had helped to steady the nerves that had been building ever since she'd learned the news.

She stopped short the minute she saw the man and woman standing in the open doorway of her shop. The man was older, with gray hair at his temples, and he wore slightly rumpled khaki slacks and a short-sleeved shirt. The woman had red hair in a French braid, and Sophie guessed that her crisp linen suit had been purchased at one of the best boutiques in Georgetown.

"Which one of you is Detective Ramsey?" Sophie asked.

"I am," the man said. "This is my partner, Natalie Gibbs."

"I understand that my shop has been broken into."

Detective Ramsey pulled a small notebook and a pen out of his pocket. "Not exactly."

"My security team specifically quoted you as saying 'break-in,'" Tracker said.

"And your relationship to Ms. Wainwright is?"

"I head up security for Wainwright Enterprises and I'm looking after Ms. Wainwright while her brother is out of town. Could you tell us what's going on?"

"Yeah." Ramsey sighed. "We wanted to locate Ms. Wainwright fast, so we gave your security team the abridged version. The unabridged one is more complicated." He shifted his gaze to Sophie. "Someone got into your shop tonight, Ms. Wainwright. They were clever enough to bypass the alarm without setting it off. A woman who works at the ice-cream shop on the corner called in a possible break-in at eight-thirty. She said she saw a light—something like a flashlight or a candle—on the second floor. When the patrol officer arrived about ten minutes later to check it out, he found the back door wide-open.''

Sophie started toward the door. "I'll need to see what's been taken."

Natalie Gibbs moved quickly to cut her off.

"It's my shop. I have a right to go in there."

"In just a minute, Ms. Wainwright," Detective Ramsey said. "First, I need to know where you were this evening from seven until nine."

Sophie felt dread shiver through her. She glanced at Tracker and saw that his eyes were on Ramsey's. She shifted her gaze to the detective. "I was attending a party at the home of Millie Langford-Hughes. I left shortly after I received a phone call from Wainwright Enterprises' security people. That was about twenty minutes ago."

"I can confirm that, Ramsey. So can Millie Langford-Hughes and any number of guests at her party. Ms. Wainwright wasn't out of my sight for more than five minutes," Tracker said.

"Can I go into my shop now?" Sophie asked.

Three people walked out of the back door just as she spoke. One of them carried a camera; another carried what looked like a large briefcase. The third man spoke to Detective Ramsey. "We're through. The coroner's office should be here in a few minutes to take the body."

"Body?" Sophie could hear the fear in her own

voice as she whirled on Ramsey. "Who? Is it Noah?"
She didn't even know that she'd grabbed Tracker's
hand until she felt his fingers close around hers.

"We don't know who it is, Ms. Wainwright. There
was no identification on the body. Who is Noah?"

She tightened her grip on Tracker's hand. "My assistant. He's a graduate student at Georgetown, and
he's been working part-time for me since I opened the
shop. He has the code to get through the security system."

"The victim is a man. We were hoping you might
help us with an identification," Ramsey said.

"Yes." Sophie couldn't feel her knees. All she
could think of was Noah lying in her shop, dead.
"Okay."

"I can do it, Sophie. You stay here with Detective
Gibbs," Tracker said.

She shook her head. "I can do it."

She knew it was going to be hard. But as she walked
up the stairs after the two detectives, she realized that
she wouldn't have made it without Tracker's hand at
her back giving her support. Even then she felt as if
she were walking in slow motion. Detective Gibbs led
them into the first room to the left.

Sophie thought she'd steeled herself, but when she
saw the lifeless form on the floor, she knew that there
was no way to prepare for it. Details made their way
into her mind like so many images flashing on an
empty screen: the body, facedown on the floor, one
hand flung up, the other at his side…the contrast of
fair hair and reddish-brown blood. She knew before

Detective Ramsey turned the body over that it wasn't Noah. But her relief was short-lived.

The man lying on the floor of her shop was John Landry.

8

AT ELEVEN O'CLOCK, the detectives' room at the police station was swinging into high gear. Tracker viewed the scene through the glass wall of a conference room. Perps were being interviewed, paperwork processed. Across the sea of desks and detectives, he could see Sophie in a similar room, talking to Detective Gibbs.

Presently, Ramsey was letting him cool his heels while he made a few phone calls. Tracker had used his cell phone to make one himself—to Chance, but he'd had to leave a message. Had whoever killed Landry gotten the coin? That was the question of the day. None of the pieces that had arrived in the day's shipment had been stolen. He'd checked that out himself.

When Ramsey had invited them down to the station, Tracker had agreed because it gave him some breathing time. He had to plan what he was going to do when Sophie figured out the real reason he was in her apartment and in her bed.

Even now, Gibbs could be asking her questions that might start her thinking, wondering. The Princess had a mind like a steel trap. And a temper like fire. Once she figured it out, he wasn't sure what she'd do, except that she'd never want to see him again.

Fear rolled into an icy ball in his stomach. From the

moment he'd seen Landry lying on the floor in her shop, Tracker hadn't been able to rid his mind of the image of Sophie lying there. It could have been her. He ran a hand through his hair as if that gesture would erase the picture from his mind. If Sophie pushed him away now, he wouldn't be able to protect her. He wouldn't be able to touch her, hold her—

Damn. He wanted to kick something—himself, for starters. He was allowing his emotions to block what he should be thinking of—some kind of strategy that he could use to keep her safe.

Ruthlessly, Tracker shoved his feelings down. Sophie had a way of scrambling his brain. He was so emotionally involved that he'd even considered the option of stepping back and assigning some of his men to protect her. But Chance had warned against doing anything that would arouse suspicion. And Tracker had already established his cover as her lover. Sticking to the present scenario was the safest option for now.

He just had to keep his head clear and focus on the facts. John Landry was dead, shot through the back of the head in one of the upstairs display rooms in Sophie's shop. There'd been no sign of a struggle. The hit had been clean, professional looking. And Landry had gained access by shutting down the security system. Tracker had checked that much out before he'd left the shop.

He glanced up when Ramsey entered the room.

"I've done some checking on you, Mr. McBride." Ramsey placed a manila file down on the table between them. "I ran this last year when we thought Dr.

MacKenzie Lloyd was missing. Would you care to look at it?''

Tracker glanced at the folder and then back at Ramsey. ''Why don't you just fill me in?''

''I know that you and Lucas Wainwright worked on covert operations in some pretty rugged places and that your service files are classified. I also know that Mr. Wainwright trusts you with the lives of his wife and his sister. I'm aware that Landry had been dating Ms. Wainwright pretty steadily for the past two weeks, but that she went with you to that party tonight. According to Ms. Wainwright, you spent last night with her in her apartment and you were with her the whole day in the shop.''

Pausing, Ramsey folded his hands on the desk. ''What it looks like to me is that something must have happened to make Ms. Wainwright give Landry the boot and replace him with Wainwright Enterprises' head of security on a twenty-four–seven basis. I'd like you to share with me anything you know about John Landry's death.''

Tracker met Ramsey's gaze steadily. ''I don't know anything about it.''

Ramsey smiled, but it didn't reach his eyes. ''Let me rephrase that. What do you suspect? And if that question doesn't suit, you can always start with what you're protecting Ms. Wainwright from.''

Tracker studied the man for a minute. Both Lucas and Mac had spoken highly of him. Rumpled shirt aside, the detective had intelligent eyes, and he'd done a heck of a background check to have dug up what he'd been able to about Lucas and his military background. How much would satisfy him? That was the question. After a moment, Tracker decided that he'd give him as much as he could. Having Ramsey on his side might pay off down the road a bit.

"There are some things I have to hold back because they involve agents working undercover. What I can tell you is that Sophie's shop is under surveillance by a couple of agencies and an insurance company or two because it's been pinpointed as one of a few stores being used by a very well connected smuggler to get some stolen coins into this country. Three of them were dug up in Turkey, and they were in England when they were stolen. Sophie is not suspected of being involved, but she could be in danger."

"That's where you come in," Ramsey said. He'd begun to tap a pencil on the desk.

"She knows nothing about the smuggling."

The tapping stopped. "Who filled you in?"

"One of the agents I can't name. He says that they're very close to closing in on the head of the ring. It's imperative that everything run smoothly, business as usual at Sophie's shop. An owner of a similar shop in Connecticut was found burned to death in his store two months ago. Six weeks ago, a woman who purchased something in Sophie's shop was killed by a hit-and-run driver."

Ramsey leaned back in his chair. "Gibbs and I are working on that case. You're saying it's connected?"

"I was told she was on her way to meet the headman. Hard to believe it was a coincidence."

"Was Landry one of the agents you're talking about?"

"Good question." The detective was smart, and Tracker was annoyed that he hadn't yet considered that possibility himself. "The other possibility is that he was part of the smuggling operation. Landry comes from a lot of money, the landed gentry kind, and a few years ago he began dabbling in the antique business for fun. He hunts down special pieces for high-paying clients."

"It would make a good cover whichever side of the law he was working on," Ramsey commented. "And you say Ms. Wainwright knows nothing about what you've learned?"

"No. I thought it would be safer for her that way. She's very sensitive…about being protected."

"I see," Ramsey said, studying Tracker thoughtfully. "How long before you can close in on the smuggler?"

"A shipment arrived today that was supposed to contain the coin. We're waiting for someone to make a move."

"Seems to me someone did. Was it taken tonight?"

"None of the pieces that arrived today were stolen. I should know more soon."

After a moment, Ramsey said, "So Ms. Wainwright doesn't know you're guarding her. You're playing a very dangerous game, don't you think?"

"Yeah. But for the moment, it's the best chance I've got of keeping her safe. I'd like to continue playing it."

Ramsey nodded. "Okay. She won't hear anything about the smuggling business from me right at this moment. But my job is to solve two homicides."

Tracker nodded. "I'll give you whatever I can once we nail this bastard."

Ramsey handed him a card. "I was thinking more in terms of cooperation. Let me know what I can do to help."

Tracker's eyes narrowed as he glanced across the room to where Sophie was being questioned. "How good a cop is Detective Gibbs?"

"As good as they get. She's been my partner for two years."

He shifted his gaze back to Ramsey. "If Ms. Wainwright decides that she no longer requires my services twenty-four–seven, I may have a job for her."

IT WAS ANOTHER half an hour before Detective Gibbs finished interviewing Sophie. Tracker paced by the elevator, feeling for all the world as if he were awaiting judgment and sentencing. Oh, he could tell himself that he'd had no business sleeping with Sophie, but he'd never regret it. What he would regret was never doing it again, never being able to touch her, to hold her.

"Tracker."

He turned slowly at the sound of her voice. She was walking toward him, and the moment he looked into her eyes, he knew he had a reprieve. She wasn't going to tell him to get lost yet.

"Will you hold me?"

He'd already opened his arms, and when she walked into them, he closed them tightly around her. The iciness of the fear that had gripped him from the moment he'd seen Landry's body began to melt, replaced by a flood of emotions he couldn't even begin to name. All he knew for sure was that holding her like this was something he wanted to go on doing for a very long time.

"I'm sorry." She tightened her grip on him. "I just can't help it. A few hours ago I talked to him at the party. He kissed me goodbye because he was going back to London tomorrow. And now he's..."

Tracker ran a hand over her hair. "I'm sorry you had to see him."

"I hate that I'm doing this," Sophie murmured, but she didn't lift her cheek from his chest.

"Doing what?" Tracker asked.

"Being weak and clinging."

"You have a right."

"But it never solves anything. It's just that..."

"What?"

"I needed this. Even when you'd dug up all that stuff on Bradley the jerk and I absolutely hated you for it, I felt better when you held me in your arms."

A flood of feelings moved through him, along with the realization that he'd felt better, too. And he knew why. What he'd felt that day and what he was feeling right now was that he'd come home. Not that he'd ever had a real one, but this was what he'd always imagined it would feel like—the warmth, the understanding, the acceptance.

"I want to take you away from this." The words were out before the thought had even formed fully in his mind. He felt her stiffen in his arms and draw back.

"I wish I could let you, but I have to stay. Detective Gibbs wants me to run a more detailed inventory and make sure that nothing was taken. And she said they might need to see me again.''

Tracker frowned. ''You're not a suspect. They can't force you to stay around.''

Sophie shook her head. ''No, but I want to do everything I can to help them find out who did this to John. He was a nice man, and he was killed in my shop. The weird part is he bypassed the security system. They don't suspect either Noah or me of letting him in. How did he do that?''

''Any security system can be disabled if the person has the right kind of background.'' Tracker didn't add that it would take talent and the right kind of tools.

''They're going to question Noah anyway.''

''They have to. It's standard police procedure.''

Sophie drew in a deep breath. ''I want you to do me a favor. I want you to help me find out who shot John.''

''Princess, Detective Ramsey is very good at his job. Lucas and Mac think the world of him.''

''He's not *you.* You head up Wainwright Enterprises' security, and you have a whole security team working for you. I figured we could go back to the shop, I'll take a quick inventory for Detective Gibbs and you could look for clues.''

''Clues.'' Tracker shook his head. He could hardly tell her that he'd already checked for them. ''You're sure you want to go back there tonight?''

He could feel her spine stiffen. ''It's my shop. Please. I need to do this. Will you help me?''

He leaned his forehead against hers. ''Your wish

seems to be my command, Princess...on one condition."

"A condition?" She raised her brows. "I don't think princesses have to accept conditions."

He grinned and for the first time all evening felt some of his tension ease. "What if I promise that there will be penalties involved?"

She smiled up at him, the first smile he'd seen since they'd gotten the phone call. His heart gave a little lurch. "Penalties, huh?"

"Only if you accept my condition. If you want my help, you have to cooperate. Once you finish the inventory at your shop, we're going to the apartment I keep at Wainwright Enterprises. I know that you'll be safe there—and I think we both need a good night's sleep."

"Sleep? If you want to get any sleep tonight, there are definitely going to be penalties involved."

"Princess, I'm counting on it."

"WHAT ARE YOUR FEELINGS about onions, garlic and cheese when it comes to an omelette?"

Sophie climbed up on a stool and faced Tracker over the counter. Chess was already at his elbow, inspecting the ingredients he'd taken out of the refrigerator. His kitchen was as small as hers, but it was state of the art. "I have very warm and fuzzy feelings for those ingredients."

The grin came then, quick and packing its usual punch. "Well, we have at least one thing in common, Princess."

The words warmed her. Up until a few days ago,

she never would have believed that she and Tracker had anything in common. Nor would she have believed that she would be sitting here in his kitchen feeling so relaxed. There was something very soothing in the quick, competent way he'd assembled a pan, a bowl and the utensils he needed on the counter between them. It made her recall the very efficient way he'd handled things in the powder room at the party.

Even as heat rose in her cheeks, she found her gaze fastened on his hands as he sliced, chopped and tossed ingredients into a hot skillet. All she had to do was look at those long, lean fingers and she could imagine them on her, moving over her skin, slipping inside of her.

"Earth to Sophie."

She glanced up. "Hmm?"

"Are you game for some hot peppers?"

"Sure." She had the feeling with Tracker she'd be game for just about anything. She could never imagine trying that black velvet ribbon scenario with anyone else. And he'd been so willing to go right along. So patient when she'd completely blown her part. And *so* skilled. She felt a streak of pleasure, just remembering what he'd done, what he'd made her feel. She'd known that he'd be intense as a lover. But she'd never thought of him as being impulsive that way or of having a fun, playful side.

Of course, she'd never pictured him in a kitchen whipping eggs into a froth. Nor could she have imagined feeling so...right watching him do it. The realization moved through her that she felt more at home here than she'd ever felt at the Wainwright estate, and a little flash of fear skipped up her spine. All her life, the people she'd cared for, the people she'd wanted to love her, had left her. She had to be prepared for the fact that Tracker would leave, too.

Unless she did something to stop him.

THE PRINCESS WAS THINKING. Tracker could tell by the small line that had appeared in the center of her forehead. The thinking would lead to worrying and then to questions. With a quick flip of his wrist, he folded the omelette over.

The last thing he wanted her to do was to start to think too hard about what was going on in her shop that might have led to Landry's death. Tracker wanted her laughing and thinking only of him.

He wanted her, period. The hunger was constant, and he was beginning to fear that it would never be sated. If he didn't do something to distract them both, he'd forget the damn omelette and take her again right now. After slipping it onto a plate, he set it on the counter in front of her. "Eat first, and then we'll play a game of twenty questions."

"Sure," she said as she took the fork he handed her and sliced into the eggs.

He watched her chew, swallow and then raise surprised eyes to his. "Marvelous. You're a pro, aren't you? At some time in your past you've done this for a living."

He smiled. "Perceptive deduction. If you ever get tired running your shop, I can give you a job in the Wainwright security department."

"No, thanks. But I'm right, aren't I?"

"I worked my way through college in a diner."

"This doesn't taste like diner food," she said around another mouthful. Swallowing, she helped herself to another one before she said, "Okay, let's start the game."

"Thomas Jefferson McBride."

She blinked and stared at him. "What?"

"We started a game of twenty questions at the anniversary party, and I thought we could take up where we left off. The T.J. stands for Thomas Jefferson."

"You were named after the president?"

He shook his head. "No. I was named after my father. I had it legally changed to T.J. as soon as I could because I hated him."

"I'm sorry." She slipped a hand into his and he gripped it hard.

There wasn't a trace of judgment in her eyes, only understanding. He felt something inside of him melt and stream away.

"He used to beat my mother. He was the reason she died when I was eleven." Now where in the world had that come from? He hadn't even told Lucas about that part of his past. Sophie was breaking down every last barrier he had.

She lifted his hand to her cheek. "It's your turn now. Ask me anything you want. I'll answer."

"New rules, Princess?"

She nodded. "A new game. Just for tonight—one question apiece. No passes, no penalties, just the whole story."

He studied her for a moment. He'd thought to distract her with the game, with the penalty that would inevitably follow. She'd raised the stakes, but the idea of learning even more about her was tempting, irresistible. "Okay. What is the very worst thing you've ever done? Something you've never told anyone else."

"Well, you don't pull any punches."

"Neither do you. And turnabout's fair play. You get the last question."

"I shoplifted when I was fourteen." She could recall the incident as clearly as if it had happened that morning. "I was in a huge department store and I was so angry at my parents. My mother hadn't even bothered to call for my birthday. And my dad was on some kind of a cruise with…I think it was his third wife. I guess I thought if I got myself arrested, I would get some parental attention." Setting down her fork, she met Tracker's eyes. "Talking about it makes it sound like pretty standard poor little rich girl stuff."

He tightened his grip on her hand. "Tell me the rest."

Sophie drew in a deep breath. "I had this shopping bag and I'd filled it with all kinds of stuff—a couple of cashmere sweaters and some pricey lingerie. I wanted to make sure that when I was caught, the charge would be larceny or grand larceny."

"What happened?"

She shrugged. "I knew that someone was watching me, that I'd be stopped as soon as I pushed my way onto the street. I got within ten yards of the door and my feet wouldn't take me any farther. I carried the bag over to the nearest counter and took out my charge card. I was too much of a coward to pull it off."

He raised their joined hands and turned hers over, then pressed his mouth against her palm. "You're one of the bravest people I know, Princess."

What she saw in his eyes told her that he meant it, and she would have said something if she could have gotten any sound past the lump that had filled her throat.

"It's your turn," he said. "Ask me anything."

He was serious. Sophie wondered if she would ever have him at such a disadvantage again. He'd told her something already that must have been very hard for him to reveal. And suddenly it was important to her that when he did reveal more of himself to her, it wasn't part of a game. "What is your favorite movie?"

Tracker simply stared at her for a long moment without answering. "You could have asked me anything you wanted."

"I just did."

He shook his head. "You puzzle me. I just can't figure you out."

She smiled then. "That's excellent. Because I always imagine that I have absolutely no secrets from you. You've seen me at my absolute worst."

"Worst? Princess, you wouldn't want to see me at my worst. I've killed people."

He wanted to shock her. She could see it in the anger that had flashed into his eyes. Was he afraid that he could somehow make her walk away? Could it be possible that he feared the same things that she did? She merely kept her hand in his and waited.

"I wasn't very good at it in the beginning. The first

time I had to kill a man, I threw up. I was just sixteen, and I had enlisted in the army with the idea of becoming some kind of a hero. I had been in fights before on the street, but nothing that involved guns. I'd never seen the kind of damage they can do to another human being. We were on patrol on one of those peace-keeping missions, and my buddy and I got separated from the rest of our unit. Next thing I knew he got shot and this other soldier was running toward us. I raised my gun and fired. The impact of the bullet... I'll never forget it."

She tightened her grip on his hand and felt his fingers link with hers. "What happened?"

"I managed to get my buddy back to the unit before I tossed my lunch all over my sergeant's shoes."

The anger, the need to shock her, had disappeared from his eyes.

"That was only the first time, Princess. There are other stories I could tell you. You should be shocked."

"I'm not." She kept her eyes steady on his. "I'm sure it makes me a very shallow person, but all I'm thinking of right now is how to get you out of those clothes."

His gaze was intense. "What do you have in mind?"

She saw some of the tension begin to ease out of him, but he was still so cautious and wary of her. Why did that thrill her right to the core? Leaning toward him, she spoke in a confidential tone. "Since I left all of the little toys at home, we'll have to improvise. I was thinking that strip poker might work. Are you game?"

9

SHE WAS A DAMN GOOD poker player. Tracker never would have guessed it because she tended to give everything away in those amber eyes. It had taken several hands for him to realize *that* was her secret. She knew people could read her easily, and she used that to her advantage.

He enjoyed matching wits with her just as much as he enjoyed testing her control in this sexual, teasing game they were playing. So far, he'd had the advantage there. She might be winning at cards, but as a result of his losing hands, he was sitting across the coffee table from her wearing nothing but his briefs and his socks, and she was still wearing every stitch she'd come in the door with.

He admired her control at the same time that it challenged him to break it. And he was making headway. She might still have her clothes on, but the pulse at the base of her throat was beating, and her eyes had deepened to that color of whiskey. They would darken even more when he was inside of her.

No. If he allowed himself to imagine how it would feel when he entered her and had her close around him like a slick, hot fist, the game would be over too quickly. And he didn't want their lovemaking to be quick tonight. This might the last time he would be able to touch her, to show her…

"I just have a full house this time," she said as she turned over her cards.

"Beats two pair." Tracker reached for the cards before she could gather them in. "My deal."

"You have to take something off first," she said, her eyes bright with amusement and something else. He knew what the something else was because the same thing was twisting inside of him.

"Fine," he said. "What's your pleasure?"

"Oh, I'm looking at it."

"You can have it anytime you want." His gut twisted tighter when he heard her sharp intake of breath and saw her eyes lower to where his erection was clearly visible through the thin cotton of his briefs. Though it nearly killed him, he reached down and ran a hand up and then down what was waiting for her.

"Tracker…" Her voice caught in her throat, and one of her hands reached toward him. He thought for a second that the game was over.

Then she raised her eyes to meet his. "Someone once told me that anticipation was half the fun."

It took almost all of his control not to reach out and grab her. When he thought of how quickly he could have her beneath him, how much he needed to be inside of her… Then she would be the winner of both games—the poker game and this new game of anticipation they were playing.

No, he wouldn't make it that easy for her. Yet. Not when she was turning his own words against him.

Drawing in a deep breath himself, he watched her tongue slowly moisten her lips, and anticipated the flavors waiting for him. But he could wait a bit more. She was here, just an arm's length away; he could reach out any time he wanted.

What was he going to do when she wasn't?

"I've never made a man strip for me before. I have a feeling it's addictive."

He could feel his skin heat as she moved her gaze over him again. He hadn't thought it possible, but he felt himself grow even harder.

"Socks," she finally said in a thin, breathless voice.

"I didn't think you were a chicken, Princess."

She met his eyes, her chin lifting. "I'm not. I don't want to end the game yet. I want to play it out to the finish."

He was coming to know that about her, too. Anything she started, she stuck to with a stubbornness he had to admire. They were alike in that, he realized. "There's only one finish to this game." He lifted one foot to the table and removed his sock.

Her eyes darkened then, going from whiskey to mahogany. "I know."

He could stop it now. Clamping down ruthlessly on the desire to do just that, he lifted his other foot and slipped off the sock. It wasn't just clothes that she'd stripped him of tonight. He'd shared things with her that he'd never revealed to anyone else, and instead of being shocked, she'd understood.

He was coming to understand her, too. He knew what it was like not to fit in, to feel that love would always pass you by. But it shouldn't pass the Princess by. He wasn't going to let that happen. As she set down her cards and rose slowly to her feet, another realization streamed through him. He'd lost more than a card game. He'd lost his heart to the Princess.

"I'm tired of the game," she said.

The words were such a crystal clear echo of the ones in his mind that, for a moment, he said nothing. He couldn't. Too many emotions swirled through him, and there was only one thing he could be sure of. He wanted her more than he ever had before. And he wanted what was impossible. He wanted her for good.

"Your wish is my command, Princess."

SOPHIE KNEW ONE THING for sure. Anticipation had nearly killed her. She wanted him, all of him. Right now. But there was something in his eyes, something beyond the heat that was piercing right to her center, and it was calling to her every bit as much as the desire that had her whole body throbbing for him.

"Tell me what *you* want," she said.

"I want...to be a part of you," he answered.

The words sounded as though they'd been torn from him, and the warmth that they caused to move through her was different than the heat he'd already kindled. She tried to tell herself that she shouldn't read anything into the words. He was merely talking about the physical act of their bodies joining. But Tracker was careful with words. He usually meant what he said. Even as a bright little bubble of joy blossomed within her, she warned herself that she was letting herself hope again for something that was impossible. And she didn't want to press him further tonight. What she wanted was exactly what she had—the opportunity to show him what she felt for him.

"Someone told me once that when you want something, all you have to do is reach out and take it."

He reached out then and lifted her over the coffee table. When he began to lower his mouth to hers, she pressed a hand to his chest. "Not yet. I'll never be able to think if you start kissing me."

"Sophie, the game's over. There's a limit to the amount of teasing a man can take."

Though everything in her body clamored for the pressure of his mouth on hers, for the feel of him inside of her, she kept her hand steady on his chest. "Slow and easy," she said, remembering the words he'd once spoken to her. "There's something I want to do first. I've been fantasizing about it all night. You won't be sorry."

She understood the effort that it took for him to ease his hold on her because she had to exert a similar one to move her hands down to his briefs and slip her fingers beneath the elastic. For him, she was going to hold on to her control. "I wanted to do this to you the first time I ever saw you, in Lucas's office—when you held me and comforted me while I was crying. When the image of doing this—" she closed her hand over his erection "—slipped into my mind, I was shocked. I'd never even thought of doing this with a man before that. But I'm not shocked now." Dropping to her knees, she closed her mouth over him.

WAS IT POSSIBLE to die of pleasure? That was the only thought Tracker's mind could seem to latch on to when he felt her lips close around him. *Yes*. The answer sounded clearly in his mind as he felt her tongue move up and down the length of his shaft. He should have known she'd try something like this. And he should have been prepared. He had to make her stop. He couldn't let her go on. He had to...

"Stop," he said, managing to frame her face with his hands and push her away. "If you want slow and easy, you're not going to get it that way."

"Right now I would settle for fast and hard," she said. "I like the way you taste."

"Good. That's good." He was amazed that his lips could move to form the words or that his hands could grip her shoulders and lift her to her feet. Then he set her back on the other side of the coffee table. "But I think what we both need is a little break. A little dose of anticipation. And you have too many clothes on. Why don't you take them off for me?"

Her fingers trembled as she closed them around the hem of her dress and began to draw it slowly up her legs. He remembered what they felt like, the smooth, soft skin of her inner thighs wrapped tightly around him. A new wave of need spiked through him with a sharpness that had him drawing in his breath. Sophie's hands paused then.

"Don't!" he groaned.

"What?" she asked.

Her tone was innocent enough, but he could see in her eyes that she knew exactly the effect she was having on him. "Don't stop."

The hem inched slowly up past her panties, exposing the silky skin of her abdomen and the narrow line of her ribs and finally her breasts. His heart was pounding, his breathing ragged by the time she'd pulled the dress over her head and dropped it on the floor. For a moment all he could do was look at her, standing there wearing nothing but a scrap of silk and a pair of strappy heels. He wanted to reach out to her then, but found that he wanted something else even more. He wanted to push her as far as she was pushing him.

"Touch yourself for me, Sophie."

He heard her breath catch, and for a moment she hesitated. Then she raised her hands to her breasts and cupped them.

"No," he said. "I want you to touch yourself right where I'm going to be, filling you and making myself a part of you."

A thrill moved through him when he saw her start to move her hand. She was going to meet the challenge he was giving her. Then he stopped thinking completely when her fingers slipped beneath the elastic waist of her panties. Through the thin silk, he could see them getting closer and closer until they disappeared between her legs.

Need spiked through him so sharply that it nearly buckled his knees as he leaned forward to grip her arms. When she put her hands on his shoulders, he lifted her over the table again. "Tell me what you want."

She met his eyes. "I want you inside of me, right now."

Tracker dropped to his knees, then pulled her to him. He seated her so that she straddled him, and pushed into her slowly. She was so wet, so tight. Feeling her stretch and close around him was almost his undoing.

"Don't move." His voice was hoarse. For a moment, he didn't even allow himself to take a breath. He didn't want this to end. If he did this right, he could make the pleasure last longer. He needed to make it last for her.

Holding her close, he leaned back until they were lying on the floor thigh-to-thigh, center-to-center. She tried to rise, but he held her still. When she struggled to arch her hips against him, he slipped his legs over hers and pinned them to the floor. He felt her inner muscles clench and stroke him.

"Let me," she said, struggling to move her hips, but as long as he held her impaled and pinned against him, her efforts couldn't bring release to either one of them. All they could bring was wave after wave of staggering, piercing pleasure. Her eyes were dazed with it, her hair like a silken fire on his skin. He'd wanted to see her like this, wanted to keep her like this. Trapped. He wanted her forever.

"Please." Her voice was a whimper.

"Tell me you're mine, Sophie." He needed at least that much.

"I'm yours, T.J."

Fastening his hands to her hips, he began to lift and lower her, thrusting in and out in a slow, steady rhythm, again and again. Each time he slowed or stopped, she would whimper against his mouth. "Again. Again."

He wanted to draw the pleasure out, make the moment last. When she walked away from him, he would have this memory of when she was his.

The instant he moved his legs and freed her at last, she rose above him. He watched her then, her skin pale in the moonlight, her hair tumbling around her face. For one timeless moment, she looked like a goddess just coming into the full realization of her power. Then she began to move, driving him as he was driving her.

As he watched her climax stream through her, he thrust upward, driving into her, and finally found his own shattering release.

Tracker wasn't sure how much time went by before he found the strength to get to his feet and carry Sophie into the bedroom. Then he lay down beside her and, cradling her in his arms, fell into a deep sleep.

LIGHT WAS JUST GRAYING the sky when Tracker slipped from his bed. She slept like a child, one hand under her cheek, the other thrown above her head. Odd that he never thought of her as fragile, especially when he was making love to her. But looking now at that narrow wrist, the delicate line of her cheekbone and jaw, he felt the need to protect grow strong within him. He wanted to continue to lie beside her and watch her sleep, but he had another job to do—the one that would keep her safe.

Moving softly, he crossed the space to the door and closed it soundlessly behind him. Pulling on his briefs and slacks, he extracted his cell phone from the pocket and tried Chance's number again.

"Mitchell here."

"We have to meet."

"All you have to do is beam me up, Scotty."

Tracker cut the connection, then punched the intercom number to talk to the men on duty. Chance knew that they couldn't say anything on a cell phone, and the *Star Trek* phrasing told Tracker that he was somewhere close to the Wainwright Building. It also made Tracker recall the days when they'd worked together for the army. Later he might smile and let himself feel nostalgic, but right now he had a bone to pick with "Carter Mitchell."

Five minutes later, he ushered Chance into the small conference room next to his living quarters. His old friend was wearing black jeans and a sweater, and a black cap over his hair.

Tracker closed the door. Then he pulled Chance around by the shoulder and punched him square in the belly. Before he could recover, Tracker jerked Chance's arm up behind his back and slammed him face first into the wall.

"What the hell—"

"I think it's about time you gave me the whole story. What kind of game are you playing?"

For a moment, Chance said nothing. Tracker could almost hear the man's brain sorting through options. He forced the arm he was holding a little higher. "Don't even think of keeping anything back this time. You can start by telling me what your real connection to Landry was."

"How do you figure we're connected?"

"There's a smart D.C. cop working Landry's homicide who started me thinking. And there are only two people that I know of besides me who could break through that security system I set up.'' He shoved Chance harder against the wall. ''The gay boy becomes her best friend, and his buddy becomes her lover—all in the interest of catching a smuggler. I don't care for that scenario one bit.''

Chance sighed. ''Okay. Landry was my partner. I met up with him three years ago. Among other things, we've been doing freelance work for Lloyd's of London.''

Stepping back, Tracker released Chance. ''And you didn't think it was necessary to let Lucas or me know that your partner who was dating Sophie and was doing his best to get into her bed was just using her as a cover for his Lloyd's of London investigation?''

Turning, Chance raised both hands, palms out. ''I told you. I had no idea that Sophie was Lucas's sister until I saw him at the anniversary party. At that point, I shared what I thought you needed to know. Hell, Landry was my partner. I had to protect his cover. Tell me you wouldn't have done the same in my place.''

The hell of it was, Tracker figured he *would* have done the same thing. He moved to the window. The job had to come first. If he was going to protect Sophie he had to remember that and block his emotions. Outside, the sky behind the Washington Monument was now backlit with pink streaks that looked like narrow, fragile fingers. The clock was ticking. ''I need to know everything you know.''

''I didn't lie to you or Lucas about the case. Landry had infiltrated the organization. His job was to pick up the item and pass it on. Only there was a problem. The item that it was supposed to arrive in wasn't uncrated. The head guy was supposed to contact him last night, and he was to join me right afterward at his hotel. I waited for him there until I finally picked up your message.''

"He was contacted, all right. And whoever did it decided to leave no witnesses. Maybe he even got what he was after. I want Sophie out of this right now."

Chase studied him. "That's one possibility. But Landry swore that the item hadn't come in."

"Why did he go into the shop unless it was for the coin? He left the Langford-Hughes party in a hurry. Maybe the coin was hidden in something else, and the head guy told him where to look."

Chance began to pace. "You may be right, but Landry may have gone to the shop for another reason. It might have been his chance to meet the Puppet Master face-to-face. There's also a chance that the item was delayed on the other end and isn't coming in until the shipment that's arriving Wednesday. That's the day that the shops on Prospect Street are having their annual Celebration Sale. The crowds would provide a good cover for our Puppet Master, and we may be able to get him."

Tracker let options sift through his mind, weighing pros and cons. It was easy to say that he was going to get Sophie out of it, but how long could he keep her safe if they didn't catch the man behind everything?

"This guy is vicious. Landry's death should convince you of that. I still think the best way to protect Sophie is to let business go on as usual. The only way to make sure she stays safe is to nab this guy," Chance said.

"With Landry gone, who's going to pick up the coin?"

"This guy always has a backup plan. They don't call him the Puppet Master for nothing."

"Yeah, well, I'm going to cut a few of his strings. The security code is being changed at the shop and at her apartment, and I'm installing video cameras. The shop will be closed tomorrow while that's being taken care of." There was something else that Tracker knew he'd have to do. Hell, he'd known it from the moment he'd seen Landry's body lying on the floor, and talking with Ramsey at the station had only confirmed it. "Two more things. I'm going to fill in Detective Ramsey and his partner, and I'm going to tell Sophie what's going on."

Chance frowned. "Those are both very bad ideas."

"Yeah. But Sophie's my first priority, and I can't let anything stand in the way of protecting her. At this point she needs to know that her life is in danger, so she can protect herself. And I prefer to always have a backup plan myself. I'm going to need Ramsey's help on that one."

THE PHONE RANG FOUR TIMES before it was answered. "Yes." Sleep fogged the voice on the other end.

"I have a job for you," he said.

"Yes." The voice was clearer. There was something in the tone. Not eagerness, but fear. "What is it?"

The Puppet Master considered, watching the play of

sunlight as it glinted off the new silver chess pieces that sat on the board in front of him. Very carefully, he moved a knight forward. ''The ceramic horse that arrived yesterday at Ms. Wainwright's shop. I want it.''

''Ceramic horse? I don't recall… No. There was nothing like that in the shipment. You must be mistaken.''

He sighed, lifting one perfectly manicured hand to pinch the bridge of his nose. The one bane of his existence was dealing with incompetence. ''I am never mistaken.''

His companion moved a rook and captured his knight. Perfect. At least one game was going well.

''I have a copy of the shipping list in my hand,'' he murmured into the phone. ''The ceramic horse is on it, along with a Louis XIV desk and an eighteenth-century harpsichord. Do those pieces sound familiar?''

''Yes. But I didn't see a horse.''

''It arrived. Your mission is to find it.''

''But—''

''Ah, ah, ah!'' He waited until there was silence on the other end of the line. ''No arguments. Should you fail, I will be forced to take certain steps. If you want to anticipate your fate, you might want to read this morning's paper.''

He cut the connection before the person on the other end could reply. Then he moved his second knight. ''Checkmate.''

He laughed softly as his opponent studied the chessboard with a frown.

''I didn't see that coming.''

It was always better that way. Destroy the enemy before he ever knows you're there. "Your mission will be a little more challenging, my friend."

SOPHIE AWOKE WITH A START. She knew even before she turned that Tracker wasn't there. A little band of pain tightened around her heart. It was silly to feel hurt that he'd left before she'd awakened. He couldn't be far. This was his home. She knew he'd be back. At one point in the night, she'd felt his arm tighten around her. She ran a hand down to her waist as if she expected to still feel its imprint.

Feeling ridiculous, she pushed back her hair and drew up her knees. When Chess joined her on the bed, she said, "He's getting to me."

The cat rubbed against her.

It struck her then that in spite of the fact that she'd been dreaming about Tracker McBride for over a year and sleeping with him for—she glanced at her watch—for about a day, she still didn't know much about him. Well, maybe she knew a little. She knew his name and that he was kind and she could beat him at poker, but in many ways he was as mysterious to her as when she'd only thought of him as The Shadow. The few secrets he'd shared with her last night had only whetted her appetite.

Somewhere in the apartment, there had to be clues. She looked around the room. It was small and the furnishings were minimalistic. Aside from the bed, framed in ebony-colored wood, the only other furniture in the room consisted of a bedside table with a reading lamp and a matching dresser. The walls were hospital-white and bare, and there wasn't one visible item anywhere that told her anything about Tracker McBride.

Slipping out from beneath the sheet, she hurried to the dresser and opened one drawer after another. She found neatly folded T-shirts, underwear, socks—all in his favorite color, black. The jeans, slacks and jackets in the closet were all either black or white.

"The man needs a little color in his life."

Chess had no comment.

"I know I'm snooping, but knowledge is power. Not that I'm finding much out aside from the fact that he's neat and he likes silk shirts." She ran her hand down one and caught his scent. For a moment it was so strong that she turned, expecting to find him in the room. But he wasn't. Beating back the feeling of loneliness that she'd awakened with, she took the shirt off the hanger and slipped into it.

"I like him, Chess."

The cat snorted.

Sophie frowned at him. "I'm telling the truth. I do like him. He's kind and gentle and funny. We have a lot in common."

Chess leaped from the bed and rubbed against her leg.

"Well, at least you agree with that. C'mon."

In the living room, the clothes he'd discarded last night were gone, but her dress lay just where she'd tossed it, and the cards were still strewn across the couch and over the floor. For a moment she stood there as vivid memories of what they'd done filled her mind.

She'd never played strip poker before. Nothing had

prepared her for the sense of power or the thrill she'd felt telling him to take off his shirt or his slacks and then watching him do it. She'd never imagined that she might be excited by having a man follow her commands. Even now she was a little shocked just thinking about it. But she'd be more than willing to play strip poker again as long as her opponent was Tracker.

As Chess hopped up on the couch, she headed for the large cabinet that Tracker had taken the pack of cards from the night before. Inside was a state-of-the-art entertainment center, and the shelves were quite literally stuffed with CDs, videotapes and DVDs. Sinking down to the floor, she began to browse.

His collection of movies certainly dwarfed hers. She ran her hands over the titles, pulling one out now and then to examine it more closely.

She estimated that he might well have the complete collected works of Alfred Hitchcock. Then her eyes widened again as she saw *Casablanca* and *The African Queen*. How clever he was to buy the classics and have them at his fingertips rather than be at the whim of cable TV stations.

"Chess, he must own every movie that Humphrey Bogart ever made!"

"I do, as a matter of fact."

She jumped and whirled at the sound of Tracker's voice. "Where did you come from?"

"My office is in the other room. Were you looking for something special?"

You, she wanted to say, and she felt the heat rush to her cheeks. Rising, she linked her fingers together in front of her. "I was just plain snooping. I guess our game of twenty questions whetted my curiosity."

She was nervous. She'd played strip poker and made wild love to this man right on the floor where she was standing, and *now* she was having an attack of nerves. How much sense did that make?

"Why don't I fix some coffee and you can ask away?"

"Where have you been?" she blurted out before she could prevent herself. He sounded so cool, as if he found women pawing through his CDs and movies every day.

Tracker glanced over his shoulder at her as he turned the flame on under a teakettle. "I had a meeting and a few phone calls to make. The security code to your shop is being changed as we speak."

Sophie's eyes widened and she gripped the kitchen counter for support. She hadn't given one thought to John Landry or what had happened at her shop since that first moment when she'd woken up. After that, she hadn't thought of anyone but Tracker. "I have to go," she said, and started for the bedroom.

"Sophie, I've sent some men to the shop to work on the security. I've also spoken to Detective Ramsey and he feels that it would be better if you didn't open today."

She whirled back and nearly collided with him. "*He feels* and *you've sent*. It's my shop. You shouldn't have—" She broke off just in time to prevent herself from saying, *left me*. Where in the world had that come from? The man had business to take care of. So did she. It was ridiculous to feel, because he'd left before she'd woken up, that he'd abandoned her. They had no claims on each other. They were just having a no-strings affair.

He took her hands. "I'm sorry."

Whatever else she might have said slipped from her mind the moment she saw he was speaking the truth. The possibility occurred to her that he was a little nervous, too, and she felt some of her own tension ease.

Lifting a hand, he tucked a strand of hair behind her ear. "I thought you needed to sleep. I haven't been letting you get much lately."

She smiled then. "I'm not complaining."

"I'm not trying to make decisions about your shop for you, either. The news about Landry will be in the papers this morning. There will be a lot of people who will drop by to browse simply out of curiosity."

She nodded, thinking. "It would probably be better to close today out of respect for John." She wasn't even aware that she'd moved until she laid her head against Tracker's chest, and her arms wrapped around him automatically. "I can't get used to it. It doesn't seem possible that he's...dead."

Sophie let herself lean on him. It was becoming far too easy to depend on him for support, and that was a weakness she couldn't afford. Hadn't she learned that lesson yet? "Thank you for taking care of it."

TRACKER STRUGGLED with the emotions running through him. Every time he held her like this, something inside of him—some vital part of himself—crept away. From the moment he'd stepped through the door that led to his office, he hadn't been able to gather his thoughts. He wasn't even sure how long he'd stood there, watching her. Perhaps it was the sight of her dressed in one of his black shirts, with the first rays of morning light haloing her hair. Whatever the reason, it struck him with sudden force that she somehow fit.

In all the fantasies that he'd allowed himself to spin about Sophie Wainwright, he'd never once pictured her here in this sterile apartment that he used when he was in the city. Now he might never be able to use it again without wanting her here. The realization moved through him like an ache, gnawing and relentless.

They both stepped back from each other at the same time. "I'll get dressed. I need to get back to the shop. I want to catch up on my paperwork and there are some phone calls I need to make. For some reason, several people in D.C. are interested in ceramic horses all of a sudden."

"I'll go with you," Tracker said.

She met his eyes. "You don't have to. I'll be fine."

He hadn't a doubt in the world that she would be. He could see that she was already gathering her rather formidable strength around her.

"And you have your job, too. This…what we have going between us…we can't let it interfere with our work."

"Until we find out how John Landry ended up murdered in your shop, you are my job, Sophie."

Tracker watched the feelings play themselves out on her face, in her eyes: a brief flash of resentment, then anger, then a touch of fear. He'd exploit that first. "It might have been you lying on the floor."

Her brows snapped together. "That's ridiculous."

"No." For now, he would have to choose his words carefully. He'd already decided on the time and place to tell her the truth. "Landry either let someone into your shop or he surprised another intruder and got shot. If you'd been in your apartment, heard something and rushed down, do you think you would have been allowed to live?"

Silently cursing himself, he watched her face blanch. Then he added, "If I called Lucas and filled him in on what's going on, what do you think my orders would be?"

"Don't call him." The anger that flashed into her eyes was easier to handle than the fear.

"On one condition."

Her eyes narrowed. "What?"

"You'll allow me to keep you safe."

She hesitated for just a moment. "Agreed."

He watched her walk away into his bedroom, knowing that her life might depend on her keeping her word.

10

"ARE YOU READY FOR THIS?" Tracker asked gently as they left the garage and walked into the alleyway that led to the back of Sophie's shop.

"I have to be," she said simply. Still, she paused— they both did—when they saw a little group gathered in the courtyard.

Noah and Chance sat at either end of a wrought-iron bench, while Chris Chandler served iced lattes from a cardboard tray. Rounding out the group were Detectives Gibbs and Ramsey, standing at the back entrance to the shop.

Noah spotted Tracker and Sophie first and hurried over. "Are you all right? The moment I heard about it on the news, I called. When you didn't answer your phone, I thought—"

"I'm fine, Noah," she assured him. "I should have called you. I'm not going to open the shop today."

"Do you know that there are men inside? They just punched some buttons and walked right in. I was going to call the police, but then they showed up."

"The men are from Wainwright's security department," Sophie explained. "They're changing the security codes."

"Smart move, my dear," Chris Chandler said, offering her one of the lattes. "You look like you could use this. Such a terrible business. And in Georgetown. I wouldn't have come by today, but Ambassador Lipscomb called me first thing this morning, yammering about some of the unique pieces that he'd heard about in your shop. Word travels so fast at one of Millie's parties."

"She's not doing any business today out of respect for John Landry," Tracker said.

"Oh." Chandler looked taken aback for a minute. "In that case, I won't disturb you." Setting his own latte down on the table, he waved his hands in imitation of flapping wings. "I'll fly away so fast you won't even see me. Just one word." He stopped flapping his hands long enough to lay one on Sophie's arm as he passed her. "Ceramics. Equestrian is good, but if anything at all comes in by that potter who made the blue-green bowl I picked up for Millie, tag it for me. I'll take it sight unseen. Can you do that for me?"

"Sure. But what if the ambassador doesn't like it?"

Chandler winked at her. "Then I'll have to convince one of my other clients that it's the one piece their salon has been crying out for." He pitched his voice lower. "I want the ambassador to know the kind of twenty-four–seven service he'll get if he chooses me to redo the embassy. He's actually talking to Beltaire." Chandler drew himself up to his full height. "Imagine, working with Beltaire when you can have Chandler. I cannot allow him to make that kind of a mistake. I'm depending on you, Sophie."

"I'll call you if I see anything, Chris."

Chandler kissed her hand. "Ta."

Chance rose from his end of the table. "I think that's my cue. Now that I see you're safe and sound, I really do have to get the gallery open."

Once Chance had left, with Detective Ramsey following, Natalie Gibbs said, "I have a few follow-up questions for Mr. McBride. Could we go inside?"

Tracker moved to the door and punched in the temporary code. Behind him, he could hear Noah say to Sophie, "I need to talk to you, Sophie. In private."

Turning, Tracker said, "Why don't you take Noah up to the apartment? Detective Gibbs and I can talk in the shop."

The moment they were alone in the back room, Natalie Gibbs flipped open her notebook. "Carter Mitchell visited the Wainwright Building at five this morning and came out an hour later. I also know that he has no alibi for last night. He says he went straight home after the party, but no one can verify that."

Tracker studied her for a minute. She was striking— red hair, flawless skin and the body of a model, only with more curves. And she was annoyed. Since Natalie Gibbs was his backup plan for protecting Sophie, he decided to sacrifice Chance. "I can tell you that Carter Mitchell is not involved in this."

Natalie's eyes didn't waver from his. "I'm not as trusting as my partner is. I also have a bigger stake in this. I want to find out who killed John Landry because I have a hunch it's the same guy or gal who killed Jayne Childress."

Tracker frowned. "Jayne Childress?"

"I worked on her case about a month ago, and it's still open. She was killed by a hit-and-run driver within a few minutes of buying a vase from this shop. I happened to be here when she bought it. She was a P.I. who did some freelance work for government agencies. That particular day, she had a job that was making her nervous. She asked me if I would give her some backup. I arranged to have a day off, and I followed her after she left here. She made a stop at the gallery next door and then she headed toward the corner. I saw her get shoved in front of a car, and the men who did it ran off with the package. Now Mr. Landry has been murdered in this same shop. I don't believe it's a coincidence. If you fill me in on everything you know, we can work together. If not, I'm going to be getting underfoot a lot. What do you say?''

What she said meshed with what Chance had said, and Tracker found his respect for the work of the D.C. police moving up a notch. Chance was just going to have to go with the flow on this one. ''I'll fill you in on everything I know, but my priority is to keep Ms. Wainwright safe. To do that, I may need a favor from you in return. I don't want her to end up like Landry and Childress.''

Natalie Gibbs smiled. ''Neither do I. Talk to me.''

CHANCE UNLOCKED THE DOOR of the gallery and punched a code into the inner door. The two detectives had arrived only minutes after he'd stepped into the courtyard himself. While it could have been a coincidence, Chance had a gut feeling that they knew about his visit to Tracker that morning.

''How well do you know Tracker McBride?'' Ramsey asked the moment the door clicked shut behind him.

Shit, Chance thought, but he didn't let his stride falter as he headed toward the front of the gallery and punched in another code for the door. "Let's see. I met him yesterday at Ms. Wainwright's shop, and we chatted briefly at the Langford-Hughes's party. Seems like a nice enough chap, but he could really use some variety in his wardrobe. I did give him the name of my tailor."

When he turned, Chance saw that Ramsey was examining one of the paintings on the wall. Chance was about to inwardly breathe a sigh of relief when the detective turned and met his eyes. "Was that why you visited him at 5:00 a.m. this morning? Because he was having a fashion emergency?"

Chance said nothing for a moment. It was an old trick he'd learned in his brief career as a cop in L.A. Nine out of ten times, your opponent would fill in the silence. But Ramsey merely waited. Evidently, he'd gone to the same cop training school. "Do I need an attorney?"

Ramsey's brows shot up. "Feel free to call one. But all I want to know is why you and Mr. McBride met this morning. I figure it has something to do with Ms. Wainwright's shop. Detective Gibbs has been watching One of a Kind ever since a woman named Jayne Childress was killed by a hit-and-run driver. She thinks you might have had something to do with it."

Chance stared. "Why would she think that?"

Ramsey scratched his head. "Call it woman's intuition. Or it may have something to do with her suspicion that you're not gay.''

Chance worked to keep his expression blank. So far he hadn't been prepared for one thing Ramsey had said. ''What makes her say that?''

''My partner has a personal interest in the Childress case. On her own time, she's been staking out this gallery and Ms. Wainwright's shop. She wears a disguise she created when she was working vice. Perhaps you recall a blond man, good-looking, fancy dresser?''

Chance remembered all right. ''Yeah, he's been in here. One time he hit on me.''

''Yeah, so she says. And when you didn't take her up on it—well, Gibbs doesn't take rejection well.''

''So she tags me for a murderer?''

Pulling a notebook out of his pocket, Ramsey said, ''Not solely because of that. Your initials, C.M., and the name of the gallery appeared in Jayne Childress's appointment book on three different occasions. One of those was the day she purchased a vase in Ms. Wainwright's shop. Did she show it to you?''

Chance masked his surprise. Jayne Childress had stopped into the gallery right after she'd picked up the vase. That had been his signal that she was on her way to meet the headman. The moment she'd left, he'd flipped the Closed sign on the door and stepped out onto the street. He'd been just in time to see one man snatch her package and the other push her into the path of an oncoming car. Their timing had been perfect. Chance still pictured the scene in his dreams as if it were a carefully choreographed ballet. Shoving the image away, he forced himself to concentrate on the man standing in front of him.

"Of course, you don't have to answer any of my questions. But my partner is in the process of making the same offer to Mr. McBride that I'm making to you—a free exchange of information."

"What's in it for me?" Chance asked.

"I'm thinking that we might be after the same bastard, and it might be helpful to both of us if we don't get in each other's way."

It took Chance about a second to decide. Since he figured that Tracker had already opened up, he didn't have much choice.

SOPHIE SET THE ICED LATTE down on her kitchen counter and turned the flame on under the teakettle. "I'm going to make a pot of real coffee. Would you like some, Noah?"

"No. No, thanks. Sophie…"

She turned to find him twisting his hands nervously. He met her eyes for a second, then shifted his gaze away.

"What is it?"

He paced two steps to the window and back to the counter. "I don't know how to say this. I wasn't going to say anything. I even thought I was mistaken, but before I left, I took a quick tour of the shop to check. I figured it wasn't any of my business. But now…a man is dead."

"If you know something, you should tell Detective Ramsey."

"I don't know anything about Mr. Landry's death."

At the sound of agitation in his voice, Sophie rounded the counter and took his hands. She'd hired Noah in his first year as a grad student at Georgetown. What he had that had gotten him the job was a passion for beautiful things. Within the first week of his employment, she'd discovered that he had an almost photographic memory, not only for people but for her inventory as well.

"Noah, no one thinks that you had anything to do with John Landry's death. I'm sure of that. What is it that you're afraid to tell me?"

"I may be making too much of it. But usually you tell me if you set something aside."

Sophie squeezed his hands. "What?"

"There's a piece missing from the shipment yesterday. You checked it off the packing list, but it's not anywhere in the store. I checked."

Sophie let out a sigh of relief. "The ceramic horse. I brought it up here and unpacked it myself."

Closing his eyes, Noah let out a sigh. "Oh my heavens. Now I feel like a fool. When I read the paper this morning, all kinds of scenarios began to run through my mind. I thought that perhaps Mr. Landry had taken it, or that friend of your brother. I even suspected Mr. Mitchell. We've never had that many people in the shop before when we were taking a delivery."

"Well, you can relax now. The horse is safe. It's right over there on the bottom shelf."

Noah walked toward the couch and began to study her collection as she measured coffee into the French press and poured boiling water over the grounds.

"Which one is it?" Noah asked.

"It's in the center. Here, I'll show you." She'd taken three steps when she heard the glass in the window at her back shatter. Acting on pure instinct, she ducked behind the end of the counter. The dull thud of a bullet sounded over her head, and she saw the edge of the counter splinter. "Noah, get out of here."

Noah was already moving, disappearing through the door as glass shattered again. This time she caught the strong scent of coffee. The first drips hit her neck just as footsteps thundered on the stairs.

TRACKER HIT the second landing just in time to see a figure come hurtling out of Sophie's apartment. Noah. Recognition filtered into Tracker's brain, and fear dug its claws even deeper into his gut.

"Sophie," he called as he reached the top of the stairs.

"Don't come in," she cried.

"Someone shot at us," Noah said.

As he moved past him, Tracker pushed the young man firmly to the floor. "Stay here and keep your head down." Then he turned to look into the apartment. When he saw her, sitting on the floor at the end of the counter, relief hit him like a low, hard punch in his gut. For a moment he couldn't get a breath. Then, grabbing on to his control, he ruthlessly shut his feelings off.

One quick glance told him that she was pinned. If she showed herself at either end of the narrow counter, whoever was out there would have a clear shot. But she was safe for the moment. Pushing away a fresh wave of anger, Tracker pulled his gun, flattened his back against the apartment wall and began to edge toward the window.

"Be careful," she said.

"Yeah." But he hadn't been careful enough. Someone had gotten close enough to kill her. Later he would indulge himself in the luxury of rage, but for now his brain had to be cool. As he inched his way along the wall, he called up an image of the row of shops across the street from One of a Kind. In the past, he'd staked out the Princess's shop often enough to have memorized the surroundings. There was a flat roof on the three-story building directly across the street, and the odds were pretty good that a pro would find it an ideal spot.

Reaching the frame of the window, he said, "Sophie, you just have to do one thing for me."

"I hope it doesn't involve a penalty."

His lips nearly curved. "Whatever happens, stay put. Can you promise me that?"

"Sure thing."

Concentrating hard, Tracker brought the image of the row of shops across the street into his mind, filling in as many details as he could remember. One quick look was all he was going to get. If he was right, the man on the rooftop would have a rifle with a sight. All Tracker had was his revolver, and he'd need a few seconds to line up his shot. Drawing a deep breath, he took a quick assessing glance around the edge of the window. He was just pulling back when he felt the heat on his cheek and heard the soft thud as the bullet penetrated the wall across from him.

"I'm all right. Stay put," he called to Sophie, and

he wanted to hug her when she did. Leaning back against the wall, Tracker brought the scene that he'd just glimpsed to the front of his mind. He'd caught the glint of sun striking metal at the right corner of the roof. He'd also caught a glimpse of Natalie Gibbs going into the store below. That meant that she'd spotted the gunman, too.

He took the time to play out a couple of scenarios in his mind. He was only going to get one shot, and to optimize his time he needed a decoy.

"Sophie, I need you to do one more thing."

"It's going to cost you."

Damn it, the woman was cool under fire. When this was over, he was definitely going to hug her. "Take off your T-shirt."

"Tracker, I don't think this is the time to demand your quickie."

This time he couldn't help but grin. "I'll get to that later. Just let me know when your shirt's off. Then I'm going to count to three. On three, I want you to wave it in the air over the counter."

"The shirt's off," Sophie said.

"One…two…three." Turning to the window again, Tracker aimed his gun at the far corner of the roof. The instant the shooter raised his rifle, he shot three times. The rifle tilted upward just before it clattered to the roof and the man holding it fell.

"Tracker!"

"You're safe now."

The next moment she sprang out from behind the counter and flew into his arms. Instantly, the fear that he'd bottled up tight began to stream away. Holding her against him, he stroked her hair. "You're safe, Princess," he repeated as he brushed his lips against her temple. For the first time since he'd heard the first shot, he began to believe that she was.

THROUGH THE WINDOW of the Beacham Art Gallery, Sophie watched Tracker in a heated discussion with Detective Ramsey, while Natalie Gibbs supervised two white-coated men who were loading the man who'd shot at her into an ambulance. Two marked patrol cars with their lights flashing had pulled into the curb at odd angles. Earlier she'd watched two uniformed men load Noah into a car to take him home. She'd never seen him so frightened. He could barely walk.

"It doesn't seem real," she said to Chance, who was standing next to her. "I know it is, but if it weren't for the fact that my knees have turned to jelly, I would swear I was on the set for a *Law and Order* episode."

"Well, it's real all right," Chance said, handing her a cup of coffee.

Wrapping her hands around the mug, Sophie concentrated on the warmth. She felt as though she'd been moving in slow motion through fog ever since that first shot had shattered the glass in her apartment. She hadn't even been afraid until she'd heard Tracker's footsteps on the stairs. Lifting one hand, she pressed it to her temple. She had to stop thinking about it, stop reliving those moments when she'd known that he was risking his life to save her and that she might lose him. He was all right and so was she.

Out on the street, Natalie Gibbs climbed into the

ambulance. Tracker shoved Ramsey aside and was about to climb in after her when two uniformed cops grabbed him.

"You're right," Chance said. "It is a little like watching a good cop show on TV."

"He was a professional hit man, wasn't he?" Sophie asked. "Tracker wants to know who hired him, and so do I." Setting down her mug, she started toward the door.

"Whoa," Chance said, blocking her way. "My job is to keep you inside. We don't want anyone else getting a shot at you."

"*We?*" Her eyes narrowed suddenly. "When did you suddenly join forces with Tracker and the D.C. police?"

"When he told me that he'd skin me alive if I let you out of the gallery." Chance flashed her a grin then, quick and charming. "I'm rather attached to my skin. And there's no reason for you to put yourself at risk by going out there, not when you have at least three competent people looking out for your interests."

"Yeah." Sophie frowned. "And isn't that a lucky coincidence." Three competent people *were* looking out for her interests. Suddenly, a dozen thoughts began to spin around in her head. Gradually they settled into slots exactly like the little numbered Lotto balls did on the night of a big draw.

Landry getting killed in her shop, a sniper taking aim at her through her apartment window—both times, Tracker had been close at hand, and the D.C. police hadn't been far behind.

Luck, the kind you made for yourself and the kind that just happened, was something she didn't have any trouble believing in. Nor was coincidence something foreign to her belief system. But there seemed to be quite a bit of both in her life recently.

Her frown deepened as she watched Tracker start conversing with Detective Ramsey again.

"Police barricades are very bad for business."

Sophie turned at the sound of Meryl Beacham's drawling voice. The woman glided forward with the grace of a cat to join them at the window. "Carter, why don't you earn some of the money I pay you by going out there and urging them to remove them? We're not going to get anyone in the shop as long as the street's blockaded."

"Right away, boss. I'll bribe them with coffee," Chance said, grabbing a mug as he headed for the door.

"What in the world is going on, Sophie?" Meryl asked the moment they were alone. "One of the uniforms told me that someone shot at you."

Sophie studied the other woman for a moment. Although they'd operated adjacent stores for the last three years, she and Meryl had never become close. But right now, she thought she saw genuine concern in the other woman's eyes.

"Someone took a few shots at me," Sophie said. "I have no idea why."

"You look like you could use a drink." Moving to a cabinet, she opened a door and took out a tray with a bottle and glasses. "I just happen to have some very fine cognac. Will you join me?"

Moving forward, Sophie took the glass Meryl offered and welcomed the liquid fire that slid down her throat.

"You don't have to tell me what's going on. It's not like we're bosom buddies or anything. And I know you live for your work, but if I were you I'd take a little vacation until the police straighten this whole mess out. In my experience, bad things usually happen in threes, and there have already been two murders associated with your shop."

Sophie stared at her. "Two murders? What are you talking about?"

Meryl waved a hand. "John Landry, and there was that woman a month and a half ago who was killed by a hit-and-run driver down on the corner. You were in England at the time, I think. According to the police, she was killed within minutes of buying something in your shop. And whoever shoved her in front of the car took the package. Surely they questioned you about it."

Sophie set her glass down. "Yes. Yes, they did. I just never made a connection...."

Meryl took her hands. "Why don't you go to your brother's place in Virginia until this all blows over?"

"I'll think about it. Could you do me a favor?"

"Of course."

"If the police come in here looking for me, tell them I'm in my shop."

11

SOPHIE FOUND THE FILE she wanted in less than five minutes. Setting it on the table in her back room, she began to work her way through the order forms, delivery receipts, and bills of sale.

The bill, when she found it, was dated May 15. Jayne Childress had purchased a ceramic vase. With very little trouble, Sophie could picture it in her mind. It had come from the shop she'd discovered on her last buying trip to England. Noah had told her that everything in that first shipment had practically flown out of the shop, and she'd visited the place again to negotiate an exclusive deal with Matt Draper, the owner. The ceramic horse had come from there, and so had the blue-green bowl she'd just sold to Millie Langford-Hughes.

Placing her hands flat on the worktable, Sophie stared down at the bill of sale. It was on her second trip to the shop that she'd first run into John Landry. Now Chris Chandler was asking her to tag all the pottery from this shop, sight unseen, and he'd asked particularly for equestrian pieces. What in the world was going on?

Closing the folder, she placed it back in the drawer

and forced herself to think clearly. Too many coincidences usually equaled a pattern.

Wasn't that the very same thing that was bothering her about Tracker? The man's job was to protect her—from the wrong men, from kidnappers, from... whatever it was that was going on in her shop? There was a pattern there too.

Clarity came in a flash of pain that had her swaying against the table and gripping the edges for support. Lucas was going out of town and somehow they'd gotten wind of whatever it was that was going on in her shop. So after a year of avoiding her, Tracker had all of a sudden become her...lover. What better way to get close enough to protect her?

Drawing in a deep breath, she pushed herself away from the table. Why hadn't she even suspected that he might be with her because it was part of his job?

This time the wave of pain was enough to stop her breath. For a moment she leaned against the table and concentrated on drawing in air and letting it out. She couldn't afford to think about him now. She had to focus on One of a Kind. Building her business was the one thing she'd done in her life that was successful. If people were dying because they'd had something to do with her shop...

Taking another deep breath, she made herself think about them—John Landry, Jayne Childress. And Sophie Wainwright?

She had to find out what was going on.

TRACKER WANTED TO PACE, but he made himself stand perfectly still while Ramsey conferred with the men who'd just loaded the shooter into the ambulance. He was losing it. For the first time in his life, he was letting the personal interfere with his work, and if he couldn't get his fear under control, he was going to be useless.

Every time he let his mind wander, for even an instant, he heard the sound of shattering glass again. Then the terror would start to build, just as it had when he'd raced up those three endless flights of stairs to Sophie's apartment.

Swearing under his breath, he turned and tried to focus on the items that Sophie had on display in her window—on anything that would stop the sound of the glass. A delicately featured china doll sat on a small, carved chair. *A princess,* he thought.

How was he supposed to think coolly, rationally, if everywhere he looked there was something that reminded him of Sophie? Scowling, he was about to turn away when his gaze was caught by the ceramic dragons, nearly hidden in the folds of blue silk that covered the floor. He counted three of them stationed beneath the princess's chair.

The whole scene was so Sophie, so one of a kind—fanciful and surprising. And the eye of the beholder was inevitably drawn to the princess sitting on her throne. Alone. He'd never thought of her as a loner, but he was coming to know that she thought of herself that way.

Out of the corner of his eye, he saw Chance approaching, and he whirled to face him. "Where is she?"

"Relax," Chance said. "She's talking to Meryl.

Ah, Detective," he continued as Ramsey joined them, "I come at my boss's request bearing gifts. She wants to know when the barricades are coming down. Murder and mayhem wreak havoc with business."

Ramsey took the coffee Chance offered him and then signaled to two of the uniforms. "Traffic will be back to normal in a few minutes. Never let it be said that the D.C. police stood in the way of commerce."

"You get anything yet from the shooter?" Chance asked.

"Gibbs is sweet-talking him now."

"I'd like a turn," Tracker said.

Ramsey shook his head. "Not a chance. You don't want to talk. You want to finish the job that your bullet didn't. If anyone can get anything, Gibbs will. One of the medics told him that she saved his life." Ramsey studied Tracker for a minute. "She probably did, too. That was pretty accurate shooting, considering that you were using a handgun."

Making no comment, Tracker glanced past Chance toward the gallery. He could just make out the two women through the glass. Sophie was safe, and he only had one choice if he was going to keep the dragons threatening her at bay. "I haven't told her about the smuggling yet. I've been waiting for the right time." He shifted his gaze to Chance. "But I have to tell her now—everything. It's her shop, her life. And she's smart. The minute she's over the shock of nearly being killed, she's going to start putting two and two together, and then she's going to give me my walking papers." He turned to Ramsey. "That's when Detective Gibbs will have to take over. I have a place in the country she can take Sophie to, and Noah and I will handle the delivery tomorrow. As far as Sophie's customers are concerned, she's out sick.''

"Sounds like a plan to me," Ramsey said.

PUNCHING IN THE NEW CODE she'd gotten out of the security man, Sophie opened the door of her apartment and stepped in. She'd thought she'd had time to steel herself, but her stomach clenched all the same. The room was dim because of the boards that were now nailed across the window, and someone had removed the shattered glass. Forcing her gaze to the shelf over her couch, she saw that the horse was still sitting there, right where she'd pointed it out to Noah a moment before that first shot.

Pushing the memory away, she crossed to the shelf and studied the horse. The workmanship was excellent, exquisite in fact. Somehow the artist has managed to capture the spirit of a horse, even the personality. Just looking at it, she could almost imagine the freedom of riding with all that power beneath her.

Lifting it down, she turned it over in her hands and studied it, frowning. If she'd put it in her shop yesterday instead of keeping it for herself, she would have charged about two hundred and fifty for it—hardly enough to motivate a murder, or two.

The sound of footsteps on the stairs had her jumping. Replacing the horse on the shelf, she raced to the door and was about to shut it when Tracker slammed his palm against it and shoved past her into the room. "I told you to stay in the gallery. How am I supposed to protect you when I can never predict what you're going to do?''

He might just as well have punched her, but this time anger warred with pain. Stiffening her spine, she said, ''That's what you're really here for, isn't it? To protect me. And you went along with...*everything* just so that you could do your job.''

''Sophie, I—''

''I'm right, aren't I? Our whole affair was just something that you agreed to because then you could do what Lucas pays you to do—look after his sister, who can't be trusted to do anything right.'' He didn't have to answer her. She could see all of her suspicions confirmed on his face, in his eyes. Pain tightened her heart until she wasn't sure she could breathe. Worse than that, she could feel the burn of tears behind her eyes.

''Damn it.'' He moved to her then and gripped her shoulders. ''I stayed away from you for a year. But you were in trouble, bigger trouble than you know. What was I supposed to do? Walk away?''

Placing both hands on his chest, she pushed hard. She might have been trying to shove a wall of granite. The next thing she knew, he'd lifted her right off her feet so that she was dangling in midair. Eye-to-eye, she glared at him. ''Walking away seems to be your specialty. You didn't have any trouble doing it in California last year. And you won't have any trouble doing it once we settle this little problem with my shop.''

''Little problem?'' He gave her a shake. ''Someone just tried to shoot you, and you want to call that a *little problem?* I promised your brother that I would keep you safe.''

''And you decided to do that by climbing into my bed!''

He shook her again. ''That wasn't supposed to happen.''

''I hate to interrupt—'' Natalie Gibbs began as she stepped into the room.

They turned in unison to glare at her.

Natalie raised both hands, palms out, as she backed out of the room. ''Sorry. I was never here.''

Tracker set Sophie on her feet hard, and she was appalled to find that her legs were trembling. She wasn't going to cry, she told herself as she felt one tear escape and run down her cheek.

''Sophie, don't. It wasn't… I wasn't… You were in danger. Damn it, don't cry!''

Locking her knees, she poked a finger into his chest. ''I'll do whatever I want. Two people associated with my shop are dead. Someone shot at me, and what I want to know is why you didn't fill me in on it right from the beginning? I'm not stupid, you know.''

''No.'' Tracker drew in a breath. ''And you're right. Maybe we should have told you. But you have a temper, and you have a tendency to take risks. Lucas and I weren't sure how you'd react. After the stunt you pulled in California last year, giving me the slip and getting yourself kidnapped, we…I decided that it might be safer not to tell you.''

''You and Lucas can't run my life.'' He had a point about the California episode. That simple fact had her temper spiking even higher. Before she could rein it in, she aimed one good punch at his jaw.

He caught her fist right before it landed, and grabbed her other hand, too. "I'm not as easy to knock down as your brother. And I won't fight fair."

She lifted her chin. "Tell me about it." For a moment, she saw something in his eyes—pain, perhaps—but her anger hadn't played itself out. "Okay, so I have a temper and I take risks. Did it ever occur to you that my character flaws might be causally connected to the way you and my brother treat me? A year ago you could have warned me that you were going to investigate Bradley instead of just letting me know after the fact. And you should have told me this time. This is my shop. Do you have any idea what One of a Kind means to me?"

"Yes."

Sophie blinked. The one word stopped her tirade. "You do?"

Releasing her hands, he took one careful step back. "Do you think I could watch you the past two days and not know how much this place means to you? I'm not stupid either, you know."

"You sure could have fooled me."

He took another step away, and Sophie felt a second tear slide down her cheek.

He raised a hand toward her face but let it hover in the air for a moment before it dropped. "Don't. Please don't. I'm going to keep you safe. In a few minutes, the man you know as Carter Mitchell is going to fill you in on everything we know. Then Detective Gibbs is going to stay with you twenty-four–seven until this

is over. I'll stay away, but I've got to have your word
that you'll cooperate.''

Her heart wasn't breaking. How could it break when
he'd just cut it out?

Tracker moved to the counter and then turned to
face her. He was still talking to her. She knew that
because his lips were moving, but all she was aware
of was that he'd withdrawn again. And he hadn't de-
nied one thing that she'd accused him of. He'd become
her lover to do his job. And when this was over, he
would disappear into those shadows he preferred to
hide in.

"—a place in the country. You'll like it, and by
tomorrow—"

What did she want with an arrogant, infuriating man
who didn't want her?

"—better pack something.''

Why had she let herself hope that something would
be different—that this man would be different? Why
in the world had she fallen in love with Tracker
McBride?

Fallen in love? The thought had her knees trembling
again. Suddenly, she was terrified that she wouldn't
be able to make it to her bedroom, and she needed a
moment by herself, to think. She took one cautious
step.

"Sophie...''

She could see concern in his eyes. Well, she was
concerned, too. She'd let herself fall in love with a
man who didn't want her. "I'm going to take a
shower.''

Wasn't there an old song about washing a man right

out of your hair? Moving in what felt like very slow motion, she made it to the door of her bedroom and shut it behind her. She'd fallen in love with Tracker. Shouldn't she have seen it coming? It had started when he'd rescued her from that balloon. No, perhaps it had started that first day in Lucas's office, when he'd held her in his arms.

Stripping off her clothes, she turned on the shower and let the icy spray send a jolt through her system. Okay, she loved him. If she kept saying it to herself, maybe her stomach would stop flipping over and she could accept it. And figure out what to do about it.

Turning the water to hot, she dumped shampoo into her hand and tried to think. Did he expect her to go quietly off to the country with Detective Gibbs while he went about the business of saving her and then disappeared from her life again?

In his dreams.

She'd been there, done that, and it had gotten her a year-long affair with a dream lover. Now that she'd had a real one, she wasn't giving him up. No way. Turning her face into the water, she let it sluice over her.

In business, she knew that there was more than one way to negotiate a deal. Rule number one, you had to know your client. Well, she knew Tracker better than she had two days ago. For one thing, she knew he was leery of close relationships. Well, they had that in common. Having abandonment issues sucked. Number two, he was ashamed of his past. Well, she wasn't proud of everything she'd done, either. Number three, he thought she was out of his class.

Men. Turning off the shower, she wrapped herself in a towel and looked at herself in the mirror. Dream lovers were a lot easier to handle than real ones. They didn't reject you and they didn't frustrate you, or drive you crazy. Well, she'd gotten Tracker into her bed and she'd just have to figure out a way to keep him there. No holds barred.

And then there was still the other little problem of who was trying to kill her.

TRACKER STARED at the closed door of Sophie's bedroom. The hardest thing he'd ever done was to stand there and let her walk away. He couldn't ever recall experiencing this icy feeling in his gut or the fire in his heart. But he couldn't go after her. It was much better to let her believe what she was thinking—that their whole affair had just been a deception he'd used to protect her. It was the one sure way he could get her to safety. Then he'd be able to think straight and do his job.

Taking out his cell phone, he punched in numbers and made the necessary arrangements. The moment he was finished, his mind spun again with thoughts and images.

He'd hurt her, but she would recover. He'd never seen anyone who could bounce back the way Sophie could. And there wasn't any other way he could think of to play it. He had to push her away so that he could keep her safe. When she was around, she short-circuited his brain. She'd nearly been killed. If he lost her...

The terror he'd felt as he'd raced up the stairs after

that first shot came rushing back, forming an icy rock in his stomach. Even now, where the coffee had stained the floor, he could picture it as her blood, and he could see her body, lying beside it as still and life-less as John Landry's had been. Tracker rubbed his hands over his eyes to erase the image.

When he turned, he saw that Natalie Gibbs and Chance had entered the apartment.

"I've got about twenty minutes before I have to get back to the gallery, and I've brought Detective Gibbs up to speed."

Tracker spoke to Natalie. "I'm getting Sophie out of this. She'll stay at my place in the country until we catch the bastard who's behind this. I want you to be there with her."

Natalie nodded.

"You won't get an argument from me," Chance said. "I can't figure out what in hell's going on. If whoever is behind this wanted business as usual at the shop, why try to shoot Sophie in her apartment?"

"Good question," Tracker said. If his mind hadn't been so full of Sophie, he would have been focusing on it himself. "Maybe he already has the coin, and he's just cleaning up the way he did in Connecticut."

"Or he doesn't have the coin and he knows you're closing in," Natalie said. "If that's true, then Sophie must pose a threat that's worth the risk of focusing attention on her shop."

"She's got a point," Chance said.

"Two points, actually," Natalie corrected.

For the first time since he'd entered the room, Tracker felt his lips curving. Beneath the detective's head-turning looks and designer clothes was a razor-sharp brain. "Ramsey was right about you. You're the perfect person to baby-sit Sophie."

"You know, my ears start to ring something fierce when people talk about me behind my back," Sophie said from behind him.

Though it was a struggle, Tracker managed not to wince as he turned to face her, but looking at her was a mistake. Whatever distance he'd managed to create while he'd been making his arrangements vanished the moment he saw her framed in the doorway of her bedroom. She stood in her bare feet, wearing jeans and a T-shirt, her hair still damp from the shower. How in hell could she manage to look vulnerable and regal at the same time? He let out the breath he hadn't been aware he was holding when she aimed her first question at Chance.

"Tracker mentioned that you're the man I *know* as Carter Mitchell. Mind telling me who you *really* are?"

Natalie Gibbs smothered a laugh, but Chance didn't miss a beat. "Your brother and Tracker know me as Chance, and Mitchell's as good a last name as any. Lately, I've been working freelance for insurance companies. John Landry was my partner on this case."

As Sophie listened to Chance lay out everything, Tracker found his admiration for her growing. The only sign of tension was in her hands: her knuckles were growing whiter by the moment. Otherwise she might have been listening to a weather report. He knew how much of her energy and her heart had gone into creating her business, and it couldn't be easy to learn that someone had used it, used her, to smuggle stolen goods into the country. And now that someone wanted her dead.

When Chance was done, she continued to aim her questions at him. She hadn't met Tracker's eyes or even glanced his way since she'd walked into the room. Odd that he found himself preferring a punch to the jaw over the cold shoulder.

"I still have one question," Sophie said. "If Detective Gibbs is right, and whoever's doing this still doesn't have the coin, how does he think he can get it from the shop if I'm dead and it's closed?"

"There's an inside man," Tracker said.

Sophie whirled on him. "Not Noah."

"It doesn't have to be Noah," Natalie Gibbs said.

Three people turned to study her.

"It could be someone who felt they could get access to the pieces through Noah. Anyone who's a good customer could probably handle him. That would include Chris Chandler and any of his clients. With you out of the way, Noah wouldn't be thinking straight. The person behind this might see that as his safest path to the goods."

"Which leaves us with our original suspect list," Chance said. "And we don't know where the coin is."

"I think I can help you there," Sophie said as she disappeared into the bedroom. A moment later, she returned with a small bottle and some cotton balls. "Nail polish remover," she said. "It's great for deactivating glue."

Her next stop was the couch. Leaning over Natalie Gibbs and Chance, she removed one of the horses and set it on the coffee table. Then she knelt down and began to work on the foil seal at the base of the statue.

"I could be wrong, but this horse came in yesterday's shipment, and I decided that I wanted to add it to my collection. I brought it up here directly from the truck."

Tracker stared at Sophie, and as she met his eyes, he cursed himself.

"If someone had just filled me in," Sophie continued, "I might have figured it out sooner."

When the foil came free, she held the hole in the base up to eye level. "There's something in there. It's taped just inside."

"Let me see." Chance leaned closer. "Yeah. I think we've struck pay dirt."

From the triumphant look Sophie sent him, Tracker knew that his plan to send her off to the country was not going to run as smoothly as he'd hoped.

DURING THE TIME IT TOOK them to get the coin out of the horse, Sophie's mind was racing.

"Pretty little thing, isn't it?" Chance asked.

"It doesn't look like it's worth killing anyone over," she said.

"According to the legend, the three coins were cast a few millennia before Christ, and they were one of a kind—one for the ruler of each of three cities along the Mediterranean. As long as each ruler held on to the coin, the cities would prosper. But greed sprouted its ugly head, and they began to steal the coins from one another, the theory being that if one brought prosperity, two or three would bring even more. Some scholars theorize that the first one to lose his coin ruled Atlantis.''

"Why go to the trouble of secreting them in statues and vases? They couldn't be that hard to smuggle, could they?" Sophie asked.

"Passing them through shops makes them much harder to trace," Chance pointed out. "Plus I think the Puppet Master likes the thrill of playing the game. This way he gets to manipulate people, like puppets."

"And he kills them," Tracker said. "My guess is that he enjoys that part, too."

"But why me?" Sophie asked. "Of all the gin joints in all the world, why did he pick One of a Kind?"

Suddenly, Tracker's eyes narrowed. "She's right. There has to be a specific reason he picked One of a Kind. The first coin was shipped to Connecticut, and something went wrong there. He had to burn the shop down. So maybe he chose a store in Georgetown because it's convenient. He may want to supervise his puppets personally this time. Sophie, you could unwittingly know the man we're after. And that's why he's trying to kill you."

"I can't imagine that I know him, but I know something about this horse. The vase Jayne Childress picked up was created by the same artist. I can even give you his name."

Chance let out a low whistle. "We knew about the shop. Landry hooked up with you there. But we didn't know about the artist. I'm going to have to make a phone call on that one. He could be in on it."

Sophie kept her eyes steady on Tracker's as she felt

her anger building. Ruthlessly, she clamped down on it. He'd be expecting temper, and so she wouldn't give him that. She'd give him cool logic. "If I'd been informed of what was going on, I wouldn't have taken the horse up to my apartment yesterday. Maybe Landry would still be alive."

In the silence that followed her statement, she rose and moved until she stood toe to toe with Tracker. "And if you think you're going to pack me off to the country while you and Chance catch the smuggler all by yourselves, you'll be making an even bigger mistake."

"You're going to the country."

She lifted her chin. "You can send me there. But I think Detective Gibbs's talents could be used more effectively if she didn't have to *baby-sit* me. And what about my talents? If your theory is right and I can somehow recognize this Puppet Master character, you need me here."

"Damn it, Sophie. I want you out of this, so I can think. I can protect you at my place." He gestured to the window. "Don't you get it? I can't protect you here."

It was the flash of fear in his eyes that allowed her to keep from punching him again. Instead, she drew in a deep breath. "Since we can't settle this in a rational discussion, there's only one other option." She pulled the two-headed coin out of her pocket. "Heads, I go to the country—but you're my baby-sitter, not Detective Gibbs."

Tracker's eyes narrowed. "And tails?"

Her brows lifted. "Tails, I agree to go with Detective Gibbs, of course."

"And you'll stay there?"

"Of course."

For a moment, the apartment was so silent they could hear the sound of a drill being used in the store below.

"Okay. Toss the coin."

She flipped it, caught it and showed him. "Heads. I guess you and I are going to the country."

12

TRACKER HAD SLIPPED totally into protective mode.
They'd been driving for more than half an hour and
he'd spoken barely three words to her.

Once she'd won the coin toss, he hadn't wasted any
time making the arrangements to get her out of D.C.
They'd been picked up by one of his security people,
and then after some tricky driving to lose any possible
tails, they'd stopped in an underground garage to
switch to another car—a sleek silver convertible.

She shot him a quick sideways glance. In profile,
he wore the grim, fixed expression of a warrior. Five
or six hundred years ago, he would have ridden a
huge, black stallion into battle. Today, she could easily
have imagined him in some no-nonsense, all-terrain
vehicle, or maybe a tank. She glanced at the white
leather interior of the car. This was the first hint she'd
had that Tracker McBride had a smoother, slicker
James Bond side to his character.

For a while, his meticulously thought-out arrangements had brought back the reality of what had been
happening at her shop—smuggling, bullets and death.
Now, with the wind blowing through her hair and sunlight pouring down, she wanted to push it out of her
mind for a while.

What easier way to do that than to concentrate on the man beside her? How was she going to snap him out of professional mode and get her lover back? Grace Kelly had had a much easier time of it when she'd lured Cary Grant into the hills of Monte Carlo.

As they rounded a curve in the road, Sophie glanced through the window and saw a valley open up below. Fields of green and brown formed a patchwork design that was bisected by a pencil-thin ribbon of silver. "Stop."

"Not yet. There's a better view up ahead."

To her surprise, Tracker pulled onto a narrow dirt road that wound its way up a hill. Trees blocked her view of the valley until they reached a clearing. Only then did he pull the car onto the grass verge and stop. A few feet away from the edge the ground fell away, and she could see the road they'd traveled up and the valley below. Getting out of the car, she moved close to the fence that bordered the drop-off. She wasn't even aware that Tracker had followed her until he said, "It's one of my favorite places."

"No wonder," she murmured. "It's…breathtaking. I love to be up high, looking out over things."

"Yeah. I figured that."

When she shot him a questioning look, he said, "Lucas told me that as a kid you spent most of your time in that tree house on the Wainwright estate."

"It gave me such a sense of freedom," she said. "I always thought nothing could touch me there."

"And now you find that freedom in your shop. You can be yourself there." He reached out a hand and twisted a strand of hair around his finger. "We're going to find out who's behind the smuggling and murders. You'll be safe again, I promise."

His gentle gesture and his understanding moved through her. "I thought you were annoyed with me."

"No. I'm angry with myself. I shouldn't be here. I should be back at the shop overseeing everything." He let out a frustrated breath. "I should never have let you toss that coin."

"I didn't give you much choice."

His eyes narrowed, darkened. "No. You've been narrowing my choices ever since I met you."

Progress, she thought. Her plan was to narrow them even more. "Since we're stuck here together on the flip of a coin, you could stay angry with yourself and I could worry about my shop, or we could honor our original bargain and resume our no-holds-barred affair. What do you say?"

She saw a mix of emotions move across his face before he could stop them. Desire, need, but she also saw surprise. It hit her quite suddenly that he'd actually expected her to just walk away from him. Could he really be as afraid of that as she was?

TRACKER TRIED DESPERATELY to clear the jumble of thoughts and feelings from his mind. He hadn't expected, hadn't thought... He'd hurt her by deceiving her, and he hadn't expected forgiveness, let alone this. She was offering him everything he wanted, and all he had to do was reach out and take.

She tapped her foot. "Do I have to toss the coin again?"

The Princess was back, and he couldn't prevent a smile. "No. My luck could turn. We'll stick to our original deal."

She gave him a brief nod, then dug into the pocket of her jeans. "You could use a few lessons in going with the flow. Here."

He glanced down at the card she was holding—good for one quickie on demand.

"I didn't have time to pack the other stuff." She gave him an accusing look. "You didn't give me time."

Even back at her apartment, when he'd hurt her, she'd intended to continue their affair. While the thrill of it moved through him, she started tapping her foot. "Well?"

"Right here?" he asked.

"Right now."

What he saw in her eyes had all of his doubts and even his surprise streaming away. All that was left was the raw need that had been building inside of him from the first moment he'd seen her. She was here. She was his. And he wanted her more than he wanted to breathe. "Car or grass?"

"Both."

"Good idea."

The sound of her laugh, low and throaty, tore at his control as he pulled her to him. Cupping her hips, he drew her up until her legs were clamped around him. He framed her face with his hands, holding her still while he savored the way her body fit so perfectly against his, center to center, heat to heat.

"Kiss me, now," she said.

He couldn't have stopped himself. Pulling her closer, he covered her mouth with his. It seemed like years since that flavor had poured through him—sweet, tart, Sophie. He'd nearly convinced himself that he'd never have it again, never have her again. He drew back long enough to drag in air and then took his mouth on a desperate journey along the line of her jaw and down her throat.

"I want you. On the grass, on the car." Each word she whispered against his skin was punctuated with a a kiss or a bite. "Again and again."

As the images and possibilities filled his mind, what little blood hadn't drained out of his head began to drum. Turning, he staggered toward the car.

"Quick." She moved her hips against him. "Now."

He nearly dropped to his knees before he made it to the car and set her on the hood. Then he fought through her clothes, pulling her T-shirt off and her bra. Unsnapping her jeans, he found her skin, hot, damp and trembling. For him. The heat building inside of him was so huge, he felt as if he were melting. Leaning down, he pressed his mouth against her abdomen as he dragged her jeans and panties down her legs. Her hips arched toward him as he nuzzled her skin, moving until he tasted her hot, sweet center. He lingered there, keeping his tongue on her, in her, until she cried out his name and shattered.

Blindly, he groped for the snap of his jeans and pulled them down.

"I want you inside me," she stated.

He entered her then—but not fully, not yet. Slowly easing her back against the hood of the car, he braced his arms and leaned over her. Then he drove himself into her all the way.

"More," she said, arching against him even as her eyes drifted shut.

"Look at me, Sophie."

She opened her eyes.

He withdrew almost completely, then thrust into her again. "Say my name. Tell me you want me."

"T.J.," she said. "I want you."

For a moment, he held himself still. If this was all he could ever have, he would take it. He would make it be enough. Even as he began to thrust into her again and again, he recognized that it was a lie. He would never have enough.

He knew the moment her climax began. Her inner muscles gripped him as if she never intended to let him go. He surrendered then, driving hard and deep until the whole world seemed to darken around him.

WHEN SHE WAS BACK in touch enough with reality to remember that she was lying on the hood of a sports car, with Tracker still on top of her and inside of her, Sophie couldn't prevent a smile.

"What?" Tracker murmured.

Turning her head, she looked into his eyes. "I was just thinking that Alfred Hitchcock always forgot to put this scene into his movies. But it was the fifties and there was a lot of censorship back then."

He rubbed a finger over her mouth. "I can never predict the odd paths your mind takes."

"Odd?"

He kissed her then, hard. "Intriguing." Drawing back, he studied her for a moment. "You're not what I expected you to be."

He looked a little wary about it, she thought. Tough. But it was hard to muster up much dignity or annoyance when you were spread-eagle on the hood of a car. Finally, she said, "You're not what I expected, either."

"I'm not?"

She shook her head. "We have a lot more in common than I thought. We like the same old movies, we're both neat, we like to drive fast little convertibles and we're both very competitive."

"We're still very different in some crucial ways." His voice had gone flat.

"We won't know until we get to know each other better."

"I can feel a game of twenty questions coming."

He sounded so resigned that she had to smile. "How about if we put the penalty rule back in place?"

He tucked a strand of hair behind her ear. "How about a lunch break first?"

She grinned at him. "Oh. Are we all done here?"

Laughing, he kissed her nose before he levered himself up and lifted her off the hood. "How about you give me the coupon so that I can use it later? The grass has rocks, and I'm not sure the hood of my car can withstand another round."

When they were finally dressed and in the car, Tracker surprised her by heading up the narrow lane instead of back down to the road. "What are you going to do? Catch fish for lunch? Or shoot a bird?" she asked archly.

The scents hit her before they rounded the curve: horses and flowers. Then she saw it and stared. The house, a contemporary tumble of squares and triangles, sat on the crest of the hill. The trees were thinner here. The top story of the house jutted above the tops of them and sun glinted off the glass. To the left, a sleek, low building in the same weathered wood as the house was tucked behind a paddock. Two horses, one a black stallion and the other a palomino, raced toward the fence and then cantered alongside it, keeping pace with Tracker's car.

"What is this place?" Sophie asked. It didn't look like a guest house or a hotel.

Tracker pulled the car to a stop and turned to her. "This is my place in the country."

Sophie stared at him. "You have horses?"

"Two. The black stallion is Pluto, and the mare is Persephone."

She glanced at the house and then at him. "You've definitely got a much fancier tree house than I do."

He laughed, then he took her hand, turned it over and kissed the palm.

"I'm going to keep on convincing you that we have a lot more in common than you think, T.J. McBride. But right now, I want to meet the horses. Who takes care of them when you're working in the city?"

"Jerry's racing down the steps right now to meet you."

Sophie turned back to the house in time to see a small man with the thin, wiry build of a jockey striding across the lawn. She felt as if she were being sized up quite thoroughly while Tracker made the introductions, and when Jerry extended his hand, he didn't smile. "Welcome, Miss." He gave her a little salute and then he was hurrying away across the lawn.

"Jerry's shy, especially with women," Tracker explained. "But he's a good cook, and he's excellent with horses. Would you like to go for a ride?"

"I thought you'd never ask."

HE POURED CHAMPAGNE into two crystal flutes, handed one to his companion, then held his up to the light. Bubbles shot upward through the pale golden liquid.

"I haven't handled the matter we spoke of yet," his companion said. "The marksman I hired missed."

"I trust you'll rectify the error."

"Yes."

He smiled and gestured toward the table. "Shall we then?" As they took their places at the chessboard, the phone rang.

Setting his champagne down, he pressed the button of the speakerphone. "Yes?"

"I know exactly where it is."

The Puppet Master let the silence stretch. "You know where it is, but you don't have it?"

"You don't understand. I can tell you exactly—"

"Silence."

The babbling on the other end of the line immediately ceased. He waited then, occupying himself by taking a sip of the champagne. The only sound in the room was the harsh breathing pouring out through the speakerphone. Fear was a powerful weapon, and he enjoyed wielding it.

"Now, if you have control of yourself, you may continue."

"I would have it for you, but someone shot at her."

When he spoke, he spoke very slowly. "Excuses only annoy me. If you want to redeem yourself for today's failure, you may have until tomorrow to deliver the item to my representative."

"I'll take care of it. I promise you. And then that's it. We'll be even?"

"That's right, my friend. I won't need you anymore."

He replaced the phone and faced his companion across the chess game. "He'll have to be eliminated."

"Of course. He's a weakling."

For a moment he studied his companion. He saw a greed and a ruthlessness that nearly matched his own, and that was rare. He'd chosen this puppet well, and the game they'd played had been exciting, exhilarating almost. Too bad it would have to end as soon as Sophie Wainwright was dead. "You'll handle Ms. Wainwright?"

"No later than tomorrow. I'm trying to trace her location right now."

He frowned. "I don't want her at the shop tomorrow."

"I'll take care of it. Don't worry."

Smiling, he sipped his champagne. He wouldn't worry because he, too, had a plan.

"GOOD BOY," Sophie crooned as she patted Pluto's neck.

"He'll keep you at that all day," Tracker warned, and just as predicted, Pluto nuzzled her shoulder. Persephone, jealous now, whinnied and pawed the ground.

Tracker sat down on the blanket he'd spread under a willow tree, and watched as Sophie moved to the mare and ran her hand over her neck. He shook his head in wonder. Sophie had not only charmed Persephone, but Pluto was also enthralled. Sophie rode well, but not recklessly. For a while, as they'd raced side by side through the fields, he's begun to believe that they did have more in common than he'd thought.

As he watched her turn and make her way toward him, he knew that he wanted to believe it more than anything. She shouldn't have fit so well in this home that he'd carved out for himself. But somehow she did.

Flopping down on the blanket, Sophie said, ''I'm starved.''

Quite suddenly he was, too, and not for food. He might have grabbed her then and used his coupon, but he could see the exhaustion in her eyes. Reining in his own needs, he began to unpack the basket Jerry had given them. Chicken, Brie, small crusty rolls, grapes and strawberries. While she spread cheese on the rolls, he tipped wine into glasses, then handed her one.

She took a sip, then, tilting her head to one side, she studied him. ''Since I was little, I've dreamed of having my own horse. Riding one—it's better than a tree house.''

''Why didn't you ever get one?''

She shrugged. ''Between boarding schools and college, I was never at the estate long enough—and then I had the shop. But you...I never would have pictured you in a place like this. I think it's definitely time to play twenty questions again.''

He could think of other games he'd prefer to play, but she was tired, and if he played her game right, he might be able to trick her into taking a nap. ''One question each.''

''That's an excellent way to start,'' she said around a mouthful of chicken. ''I'll begin. What's your favorite Christmas memory?''

''My what?''

She met his eyes. ''I can ask you something on any

topic I like. If you pass, there's a penalty.''

His eyes narrowed. "I know the rules. I'm just trying to think." Leaning back against the tree, he searched his memory. Christmases past. Many of them he'd spent alone, hardly bothering to note the date on the calendar. Even last year, when he'd moved in here, he'd been alone. Mac and Lucas had invited him, of course, but he'd declined because Sophie would be there.

Pushing the memory away, he dug deeper. "I'd have to say it was the Christmas I met Jerry. We were both working on a horse farm in Kentucky. He was a trainer, and I needed work." Tracker grinned. "I was fifteen and cocky, and the job he gave me was a lot more work than I'd anticipated. He was a perfectionist, never satisfied with anything I did, and it became my goal in life to please him, just out of spite. He also found me a spot to bunk in the barn. Christmas that year, he dragged me to his place. He said that no one should be alone at Christmas, and since we both were, we'd have to put up with each other. Shortly after that, he ordered me to move in with him. It's a wonder we didn't kill each other."

"Has he been with you ever since?" Sophie asked,

Tracker shook his head. "I went back to Kentucky to find him when I decided to take the job Lucas offered me."

"You figured you owed him," Sophie said.

"I didn't think of it that way. Neither did Jerry. I knew I wanted a place with horses, and I needed someone to look after them. Jerry fit the bill. It had been about ten years since I'd seen him, and he hadn't changed a bit. He's still as cantankerous as ever."

Sophie yawned as he refilled her glass. "Your turn."

He thought for a minute, then said, "What's your favorite Christmas memory?"

She took a sip of the champagne. "That's an easy one."

He figured it would be. There had to be so many happy memories to choose from.

"I was five and both my parents were away. It was shortly after they'd divorced, and Lucas had decided to stay at school. It was the night before Christmas, and I was at the Wainwright estate with a nanny and the servants, and I heard Santa's reindeer land on the roof."

"You thought you heard them?"

"No," she said firmly. "I really heard them. Knowing that they were real and that at least Santa hadn't forgotten me was the best Christmas present I got that year."

Tracker took a sip of his own champagne as he tried to picture Sophie as a five-year-old, alone for the holiday except for imaginary reindeer. Maybe they did have as much in common as she thought. The possibility sent a little flash of panic skipping through him.

"My turn again," she said.

"Oh no. We agreed one each."

Her eyes widened. "You said one each. I don't recall agreeing. Besides, answering that first question wasn't so painful, was it? And if we keep playing twenty questions, I won't spend the time worrying about what's going to go on at my shop tomorrow."

His eyes narrowed. "I can see why you're such a success at business. You're a very sneaky negotiator."

She smiled at him. "Count on it. Now, tell me about your first sexual experience."

He swallowed wine fast before he choked on it. "No way."

"Chicken."

"You can't expect me to remember—"

"Everyone remembers the first time. Was it that horrible? Weren't you successful?"

"Of course not. I mean, of course I was." Then he narrowed his eyes. She was baiting him on purpose so that he would tell her.

She held out a hand, palm up. "If you tell me about yours, I'll tell you about mine."

"Bait and trap," he said, shaking his head.

"Whatever works."

There was more than one way to play this game. Setting his glass of champagne on level ground, he stretched out on the blanket beside her. "Marylee Jazinski."

"See, you do remember."

"Every detail."

"Was she pretty?"

Tracker tried to summon up an image, but it was blurred. "She was a blonde. I vaguely remember hair the color of wheat bleached by the sun." Reaching out, he twisted a strand of Sophie's hair around his finger. "Since I was about sixteen at the time, I was drawn to her other, fairly amazing, attributes."

"I'm sure."

"She was an older woman and very experienced."

"Really?"

The dry tone nearly had him smiling. "She hired me to give her riding lessons, and she confessed to me she'd wanted me the first time she'd seen me."

"That old line."

He tucked the strand of hair behind Sophie's ear and gave in to the temptation to run his finger down her throat. Her pulse began to speed. "Worked for me."

"If she was older, it probably happened in a bed, then?" Sophie asked.

Tracker cleared his throat. "Eventually."

Her eyes narrowed. "Do I have to beat the details out of you?"

"Do you really want them? I think I'm detecting a note of jealousy in your tone." And not just jealousy, he thought, but excitement, too.

"Don't be ridiculous. Why should I be jealous of an older woman who took advantage of you?"

He pressed a finger against her lips and held it there. "That wasn't the way it was. She initiated me into the art of lovemaking."

When Sophie rolled her eyes, he nearly laughed. Her dry sense of humor was a constant delight to him. Very slowly he drew his finger down her lips to her chin. "All I knew up to then I'd read in books."

"You were sixteen and you'd already read books?"

"Quite a few. What they tell you about teenage boys and hormones is absolutely true. I'd seen some movies, too. But it wasn't like the real thing." Keeping his eyes steady on hers, he settled his hand at her throat and leaned closer until his lips were close to her ear. "Would you like me to tell you exactly what she asked me to do to her, Sophie? Would that excite you?"

The pulse at the base of her throat raced against his fingers.

"Yes, I can see that it would. Would you like me to show you what she asked me to do to her that day?"

Raising his head, he saw that her eyes had deepened to that darker color that always aroused him.

She placed her hand on the side of his face. "I want you to kiss me."

"I can't. Marylee would never let me kiss her on the mouth until I had undressed her." He was almost sure that was a lie, just as most of what he was saying was a lie, but he knew that if he kissed Sophie now, his control would begin to slip as it always did. The temptation just to lose himself in her was so great. But the game that he'd begun was arousing them both. He wanted to see where it would lead and where he could take her. Grasping her hand, he placed it on the blanket.

"She would always lie very still and just tell me what to do. First I would take off her shirt and bra." Slowly, taking his time, he eased Sophie out of both. "She always wanted me to touch her breasts. Sometimes she'd tell me to do this." He began to circle one slowly with his finger, over and over until the tip of it grew hard and her hips began to move. Then he caught the nipple between his thumb and forefinger and squeezed.

When Sophie moaned and her hips arched upward, he began the process again on the other breast. "She loved to have me play with her breasts, but I was always impatient to see her naked." He dragged one finger slowly down Sophie's stomach and then along the skin just beneath the edge of her jeans.

When she began to tremble, he lingered, brushing his hands over her again and again, determined to test them both. Her voice was strained when she finally said, "Tracker, please."

"Please what?"

"Undress me the rest of the way. I want you inside of me. Hurry."

He leaned down then to blow on the skin that he'd sensitized with his fingers, and she arched her hips upward. Then slowly he unsnapped her jeans and drew the zipper down, letting his finger rest right where the zipper ended.

"Hurry," she said. "I want you."

"But you wanted to know what my first time was like, Sophie. It's your game, your rules."

Inch by inch he dragged her jeans down the length of her legs, trailing his fingers after them, stopping to trace patterns on her inner thighs, the backs of her knees. "I love your legs, so strong, so smooth."

The moment he spoke the words, her muscles went lax. It surprised him how much he loved seeing her this way, limp and totally his. Even as the punch of power moved through him, his mind remained focused totally on Sophie and what he could do for her. How much more pleasure could he give her? How much further could he drive them both?

He brushed his fingers over the arch of her foot and then up her calf. "Do you like that, Sophie?"

"Yes." Her voice was soft, barely a whisper, but it sent ribbons of heat curling along his skin.

"And here?" Keeping his touch featherlight, he moved his hand up the inner side of her thigh. "Do you like this?"

"Mmmm." She arched toward his hand once, then again. Spreading her thighs, he knelt between them and ran one finger down the satiny panties that formed the only barrier between his finger and her center. She was already wet for him and hot. "And this?"

"Tracker, I—please."

"Please what? This?" He drew his finger down her again, and again, increasing the pressure just a little each time. When the first climax tore through her, he very nearly climaxed, too.

Then, lying down beside her, he gathered her close and just held her until the shuddering stopped. He needed to take a moment for her, and just as much for himself. If he entered her now, he'd be rough again, and he wanted desperately to be gentle.

She lifted her head and said, "Come inside me now. Please. I need you."

Whatever resolve he'd managed to gather scattered away, and his own need rushed in to fill its place. He fumbled with his clothes, and when he was finally free of them, he shifted to his back and she straddled him. Gripping her hips, he held her still for one moment, allowing her to fill his vision, his world. Then, lifting her, he plunged into her and watched pleasure cloud her eyes.

The moment she began to move, his vision began to blur. *Not yet.* He gripped her hips again.

"*Let* me." She struggled, but he held her in place. "I want…"

With one hand, he touched the spot where her body joined his.

Crying out, she arched her back as another climax rushed through her. He'd never seen anything more beautiful, more arousing. When she collapsed on top of him, he held her tight. And he knew that he could have gone on holding her for a long while.

But she began to rock her hips against him as she captured his mouth, breathing his name. "Tracker, I want you to come for me now."

Rolling her beneath him, he thrust once, then again, and poured himself into her.

13

NATALIE GIBBS TOOK OUT a handkerchief and wiped at the seat of the booth before she sat down. "Did anyone ever tell you that you have deplorable taste in restaurants?"

"This isn't a date," Chance said. If it were, he might have tried to figure out why the woman sitting across from him rubbed him the wrong way.

"Thank heavens for that. You're not my type."

He was going to stick to business. They were going to share what they'd found out and coordinate their plan for tomorrow, and then drive out to Tracker's place and fill him in. But Chance found himself saying, "You could have fooled me. Ramsey told me you were the blond boy who hit on me that day in the shop. That was a hell of a risk to take. What would you have done if I'd taken you up on it?"

She smiled at him. "Not much of a risk when you think about it. If you were straight, you wouldn't have been interested. If you were gay, you would have ended up disappointed." Her smile faded. "I was checking out who worked in the gallery. It was the last place Jayne Childress stopped before she was killed. The first minute I looked at you I didn't think you were gay."

His frown deepened. He didn't like it one bit that she'd seen through him. "Why not?"

Head tilted, she studied him for a minute. "A feeling. I felt it the first time I walked into the gallery and our eyes met."

It occurred to him that he knew exactly what she was talking about because he was feeling it right now—a little shock of recognition that registered like a quick punch in the gut.

"What'll you have, sugar?"

Glancing up, Chance saw that the waitress was talking to Natalie.

"Long time no see, Mae. Can you hazard a guess as to how long ago that pot of coffee was made?" Natalie asked.

Chance noted that the waitress was not wearing a name tag. The woman, who was short, stocky and in her early fifties, glanced to the counter at the coffee-maker, then leaned closer to Natalie. "I think the Beatles were still making records."

Natalie laughed. The full, bright sound had Chance experiencing that low punch in the gut again.

"Thanks, Mae. I'll take a diet soda with a twist of lemon, if you have it."

"Make that two." As soon as Mae ambled out of earshot, he said, "You've been in here before."

Her brows shot up. "That's how I know you have deplorable taste in restaurants. When I was a beat officer, my partner loved this place. I learned the hard way to avoid anything that doesn't come right out of a bottle or a can."

Chance found himself wondering how she would

look in a uniform. Squashing the image, he pulled out his notebook. When he glanced up, he saw that Natalie had taken hers out of her purse and was uncapping an expensive-looking monogrammed pen. "Shall we get down to business?" she asked.

"Right. Bad news. I just learned that the artist who created the ceramic vase and horse and the owner of the shop that exported them to One of a Kind are both dead."

Natalie stared at him. "Have you let Tracker and Sophie know?"

"I'll fill them in when we get there. It's the kind of news I'd rather deliver in person." For the first time, Chance realized that he'd waited because he'd wanted to talk to Natalie first, to get her input.

Tapping her pen on the notebook, she frowned. "I don't like it. Whoever we're dealing with takes no prisoners." She met his eyes. "I want to get him."

"Did you find out anything more about the shooter?"

Natalie smiled. "I made him an offer he couldn't refuse. His attorney called and wants to meet first thing in the morning. I'm betting we'll have a name by the time Sophie opens her shop."

Mae arrived with their drinks, and as soon as she left, Natalie said, "I also paid a visit to Noah Danforth. He had the shades down in his apartment and was pleading a migraine. I think someone put the fear of God into him. What's your take on Meryl?"

"She's clean as far as I can see. Why?"

Natalie tapped her pen thoughtfully. "The proximity of the shop to Sophie's is interesting. It's provided the perfect place for you to spy on Sophie. It would be useful for anyone who was waiting to pick up those coins.''

''But she's seldom around. She only dabbles in running a business.''

Natalie slid out of the booth. ''We'd better hit the road. I'll drive. I've seen your car.''

''GOOD WORK,'' he murmured into the phone. ''Excellent. I'll have to give you a bonus for this.''

As the voice on the other end of the line continued, outlining the details, he had to admit it seemed foolproof. It really was so easy to trace calls made on cell phones nowadays. And he could rest assured that Sophie Wainwright would not appear at her shop tomorrow.

He smiled at his reflection in the mirror. The Puppet Master would be able to supervise the last part of the game himself.

After slipping into his jacket, he plucked a rose out of a vase, broke off the stem and slipped it into the buttonhole of his lapel.

Then he would have to be very careful to clear the chessboard. He hadn't gotten to where he was by leaving any loose ends.

THROUGH THE GLASS DOORS that opened onto a balcony, Sophie could see that the sky was graying, the day slipping away. Just as Tracker was slipping away.

No. She pressed a hand against the small bubble of fear that had formed in her stomach when she'd awakened in his bed and found him gone. It was ridiculous to feel abandoned. There were phone calls he had to answer, arrangements he had to make for tomorrow.

She was being paranoid, but she couldn't rid herself of the fear that he was withdrawing from her again and that the afternoon they'd just shared had been some kind of going-away gift to her. When they'd come back from their ride, he'd taken her to bed, and his lovemaking had been so different, so sweet and unhurried. He'd made her feel fragile, treasured, loved.

Loved. She hugged the word to her for a moment. Then she glanced at the empty bed and the rumpled sheets. And now he was gone.

When she heard the phone ring, she thought it might be Tracker checking on her. But after picking up the extension on the bedside table, she figured out it was her cell and dug it out of her purse. "Hello?"

"Sophie, are you all right?" Mac demanded immediately. "Lucas just finished talking to Tracker. We heard the news about John Landry when we came into Key West for dinner."

"I'm fine," Sophie said as she sank onto the edge of the bed and tried to gather her thoughts.

"Lucas told me that Tracker is handling everything, but I just had to hear your voice."

And it sounded strained, even to her own ears. Focusing, Sophie tried for an annoyed tone. "Thanks to Tracker, I can't go into my shop without tripping over Wainwright security men."

"Good," Mac said. "You can depend on him to take care of you. But I told Lucas we should cut our trip short."

"Absolutely not. There's nothing that you could do."

Mac sighed. "Well, I could make sure that you're not alone. You could stay with us at the town house. I keep thinking of you all alone in that apartment."

Sophie glanced around the room. "I'm not there. I'm at Tracker's country place."

There was a beat of silence before Mac said, "*Well.* Lucas and I have never been invited to his country place. Things must be going pretty well between the two of you."

It hadn't occurred to Sophie until that moment how much she'd really missed having Mac around to talk to. "I don't know how well things are going. One minute they seem great. He's so kind and romantic."

"Romantic? Now I'm jealous," Mac said.

Sophie laughed and felt some of her tension ease. "Yeah, right, like you haven't turned my brother into a mush ball."

Mac sighed again. "I know. But Tracker has never impressed me as the romantic type."

"No. The problem is he's romantic one minute, then he pulls away the next."

"That doesn't surprise me considering what happened to him as a kid. He doesn't talk about it, but after his mother died, he was put into the foster care system. He got into a lot of fights and that meant he was moved around a lot. He told Lucas once that his father was a violent man, and he was afraid his temper meant that he'd inherited some of his father's tendencies."

"Mac, he's the gentlest, kindest man I've ever known."

"Then all you have to do is have the patience to convince him of that."

Sophie leaned back with a sigh. Patience had never been her long suit. "You know, this whole thing was easier when all I was going to do was play some games with those sex toys of yours."

Mac laughed. "Yeah. Sex is the easy part. But don't get discouraged when he pulls away. Your brother once left me in a hotel room in Key West and I didn't think I'd ever see him again."

"Really? What did you do?"

"I went after him."

TRACKER LET NATALIE GIBBS and Chance in the front door just as Sophie descended the wide sweep of stairs in the foyer of the house. He felt her accusing gaze at the back of his neck before he turned to face her. "We're having a strategy meeting," he said.

Her brows shot up. "I thought we agreed that I would be filled in on everything from now on."

"Of course. I didn't tell you they were coming because you needed the rest. But we're going to need all the brain power we can get for this." His voice sounded stiff, formal. He was still angry with himself because he hadn't really wanted to leave her in his room to rest. When they'd come in from the stables, he'd taken her there, intending to let her sleep. But he hadn't been able to leave. Worse than that, he hadn't been able to keep himself from touching her and then making love to her. Even when she'd fallen asleep, he'd barely been able to summon up the will to leave the room. But she'd needed the rest, and he'd needed to clear his head.

Now he could see in her eyes that she was annoyed. That was good, he told himself. It would help both of them maintain some distance. Even as he reminded himself of that, he moved to her and took her hand. Her annoyance faded immediately, and beneath it he saw the hurt. Before he could even think to stop himself, he leaned forward and brushed his lips across hers. "There's bad news, Sophie. We'll go into the living room, and Natalie and Chance can fill you in."

An hour later, Tracker made himself lean back in his chair and concentrate on easing the tension out of his shoulders. Sophie had taken the news of the two deaths in England very well, and she was proving to be a very active participant in their strategy session. It was at her suggestion that they'd narrowed their suspect list to people who had been at Millie Langford-Hughes's party and had mentioned ceramic pieces.

They'd placed the names on separate folded sheets of paper and lined them up like place cards. Millie Langford-Hughes, Sir Winston Hughes and Chris Chandler. Natalie had insisted that they make a card for Noah, and they'd marked Chandler's card with a star to indicate that the Puppet Master might be one of his customers.

Tracker shifted his gaze to Sophie's two other interrogators. They worked surprisingly well together, considering how different their approaches were. Natalie Gibbs had a razor-sharp mind that worked in a relentlessly linear path, while Chance's mind seemed to hopscotch all over the place. Together, they'd grilled Sophie pretty thoroughly on everything she could recall about the buying trip she'd made to the British Isles in the middle of May.

Sophie pressed her fingers against her eyes. "Yes, there were customers in the shop that day, but I was concentrating on business." She pressed a hand to her temple. "I don't think I could describe one of them if I tried. I remember John Landry because he talked to me."

"Close your eyes," Natalie suggested. "Try to picture them as if they're in a movie you're playing in your mind."

Sophie leaned back in her chair. "There was a family with a little boy. He wanted to touch everything, and every time his parents looked away, he did. He would have broken a vase if this woman hadn't grabbed it when it dropped from his little hands."

"What did she look like?" Natalie prompted.

"Stocky, and she wore a wide-brimmed hat. She laughed to reassure the little boy—a deep laugh, and she had large hands. I remember thinking that when she caught the vase. And that's all I can remember."

"Let's try a new tack," Tracker suggested. "I'm willing to bet that whatever triggered the killing spree happened the night of the party. The third coin was supposed to arrive that day. What if the Puppet Master was tempted to get a little too close this time and someone, perhaps John Landry, spotted him?"

Chance rose and began to pace. "That might explain why he left in such a hurry."

"He seemed excited when he said goodbye to me,"

Sophie said. "I asked him what was wrong and he said something about seeing a stranger who looked familiar."

"Anything else?" Tracker asked.

"He was flying back to England the next day."

"That means he was pretty sure that we'd have everything tied up by then," Chance said.

"Backtrack a little. Can you remember what you were talking about before he mentioned the familiar-looking stranger?" Tracker asked.

Sophie thought for a minute. "He came over to say goodbye, and then...we got to talking about the ceramic pieces. He mentioned that Matt Draper wanted to know if I'd gotten the horse. I forgot all about that."

"Can you remember what you told him?" Tracker asked.

Sophie met his eyes. "I told him that I'd liked it so much I'd taken it right upstairs to uncrate by myself. I'm sorry I didn't remember that before."

"*Upstairs.* If you didn't mention your apartment specifically, he may have thought you uncrated the horse in the second-floor display room, and he might have gone to get it," Tracker said.

Chance sat back down at the table. "Okay. He saw someone he thought he recognized, and he thought he knew where the piece was, so he had the perfect bait to lure the Puppet Master out into the open." Chance glanced first at Tracker and then at Sophie. "Who did he talk to before he left the party?"

Tracker shook his head. He'd seen Landry kiss Sophie on the cheek, and had felt a stab of jealousy. All he could recall was walking across the room to deliver the quickie coupon to Sophie. All he'd been thinking of was her.

Sophie frowned. ''He could have talked to anyone on the way out.''

''Or he could have set up the meeting after he left. We're no closer than we were an hour ago,'' Chance said.

Glancing at her watch, Natalie Gibbs rose from the table. ''We better hit the road,'' she said to Chance. ''I'd like to run a few things down at the office, and then I'm going to go to bed and give my subconscious a chance to mull this stuff over.''

''Good idea,'' Sophie said.

Chance rose and walked with Natalie toward the door. ''I can think of a lot more interesting things to do in bed besides mull.''

''I'm sure you could, but then you'd run the risk of blowing your cover, hotshot.''

''Ouch,'' Chance said as he pulled an invisible knife out of his chest.

FOR A FEW MINUTES after they left, Tracker was busy on the phone, and Sophie used the time to rearrange the place cards on the table. There was a thought tickling the edges of her mind. It had been nagging at her like an itch just out of reach since... If she could remember exactly when it had started, she might be able to grasp it. Frowning, she thought hard. Nothing.

''What is it?'' Tracker asked.

She pressed a hand to her temple. ''I don't know. Something that we were talking about...it's just out of reach. I'll remember when I'm not thinking so hard.''

"You should get some sleep. I have more arrangements to make.''

Sophie felt a band tighten around her heart. So they were back to formality, were they? She'd just see about that. Rising, she moved until she was behind his chair and then placed her hands on his shoulders. "If you're thinking about making some big sacrifice and sleeping on the couch over there, I'll come down and find you.''

"Sophie, you need the sleep, and so do I. I need to be sharp in the morning. I want to get this bastard.''

For a moment she said nothing. His selection of the singular pronoun hadn't escaped her. She carefully lifted her hands off of him before she gave in to the urge to choke him or, better yet, box his ears. Oh, she should have seen it coming. He was becoming as easy to read as a kid's book. But she'd been blinded by him, softened by the day they'd just shared and what she was coming to feel for him. And he'd probably done it all on purpose. For that possibility alone, she was going to make him pay. Later. Right now, she had a deal to close and it was going to take a cool head.

Drawing in a deep breath, she took a careful step back and clasped her hands behind her back for good measure.

"I never thought you were a welsher,'' she said.

He twisted around in his chair. "What?''

"We struck a bargain.''

Fury flared into his eyes as he rose and sent his chair flying. She took a quick step back.

"What are you talking about? I've kept my part of our bargain. I agreed to your rules—I've played all your games. Hell, it's bad enough I can't keep my hands off of you. I can't get you out of my head. I can't get you out of my dreams. What more do you want?"

Satisfaction streamed through her. It wasn't noble, but right now she was glad that she'd made him suffer.

He gripped her arms and lifted her off the floor. "What do you want? Do you want me to make love to you right now, right here? Do you want me to make love to you in every room in the house?"

Sophie was very much afraid that she did. *Later,* she thought. They were going to get some things settled first. But with his eyes burning into hers, she wanted him more than she wanted to breathe.

"I can't stop wanting you," they both said simultaneously.

He already had her against the wall, his hands unsnapping her jeans, dragging them down. She just managed to hear his groan above the thunder of her heart as she gripped him and guided him in.

"I can't stop wanting you." Holding her hips, he thrust in and drew out.

His face filled her vision. He was angry, desperate, and he was hers.

"Damn you, Sophie." He thrust in again, withdrew and thrust again.

"I need you."

This time they spoke together as she fisted her hands in his hair and brought his mouth to hers. They were

both going to have to get used to it. That was the last
rational thought she had before the world spun away.

WHEN SHE OPENED HER EYES, she found she was lying
on top of him on the floor. Raising her head, she tried
to read the expression on his face. *Stunned. Staggered.*
Those were the two words that came to mind. They
were the same words she would have used to describe
how she was feeling, too.

He raised a hand to her cheek. ''Are you all right?''

''Fabulous.''

But he didn't smile. He just studied her as she'd
been studying him. ''I—I'm not usually…'' He paused
as if searching for a word. ''I'm not usually like a…''

''Rabbit?''

He laughed then, wrapping his arms around her. ''I
was thinking more of a teenager with raging hormones, but I guess *rabbit* will do.''

''Well, I've never been like a rabbit, either.'' She
grinned at him. ''But why should they have all the
fun?''

They both laughed then until they were winded and
weak. When their eyes met and held she felt closer to
him than when they'd been making love.

''T.J.—'' she began.

''Sophie—'' he murmured at the same time.

''Go ahead,'' Tracker said.

She had to bite down on the inside of her cheek to
keep the words from spilling out. *I love you.* He wasn't
ready to hear that. She wasn't sure she was ready to
say it, not with panic pounding up her spine. Thank
heavens for fear and its very sobering effect.

TRACKER CONTINUED to stare at her as the silence stretched. What he'd nearly blurted out was only crystallizing in his mind. Thinking it, knowing it, was one thing. But saying it—he couldn't allow himself to do that. Not yet.

"We have to talk."

"No," he said as a ribbon of sheer panic uncoiled through his veins.

"Well, then I have to talk. All you have to do is listen." After levering herself off of him, she began to search for her clothes. "But first, I'm going to get dressed and so are you, so we don't turn into rabbits again."

"Good point," he said as he gathered his clothes and struggled into them. He needed time to think, and that just wasn't going to be possible as long as she was lying on top of him naked.

"I'll sit on one side of the table and you sit on the other," she said.

He grinned then. "If you think that's going to help…"

"Any port in a storm." She ran a hand through her hair, trying to straighten it, and he found himself charmed by the simple, feminine gesture.

"I'm going into the shop with you tomorrow."

He forced himself to focus. "That's understood."

She glared at him. "Do you think I'm stupid?"

"No."

"Then don't think you can fool me by parsing your sentences. 'That's understood!' Baloney! Natalie and Carter—I mean, Chance—were here for over an hour, and nothing was mentioned about tomorrow. And a few minutes ago you said '*I* have to be alert at the shop tomorrow.' *I* not *we*. I know you have some plan up your sleeve to leave me behind, and I could come up with a better one to foil it. But I'd rather focus on catching this guy so I can get back to my shop and a normal life.''

Tracker sighed. Had he really thought he could fool her? ''Sophie, I promised Lucas I would keep you safe. This guy is smart and lethal. I don't want you near him.''

She moved around the chair, then placed both hands flat on the table and leaned toward Tracker. ''Our only chance of catching him is if I'm in that shop tomorrow. For whatever reason—greed, arrogance, love of the game—he's going to be there tomorrow. I know it.''

Tracker faced her across the table, determined to hold his ground. ''All the more reason for you to stay away and let Gibbs and Chance and me do our job. You'll be in our way.''

He watched the hurt flash into her eyes and felt it slice through him.

''I have to be there because I might be able to recognize him.''

''How? No one has seen him. He may even be a she.''

''When John Landry talked to me about seeing a stranger who looked familiar, I remember that I'd had the same impression at the party. It was fleeting, and I can't remember who it was. But if I see that person again, I think I'll remember. That could be why someone is trying to kill me.''

She was making sense, and Tracker didn't like it one bit. If there was a chance that she could finger the guy, then they could get him.

"Otherwise, he could slip right through your hands, and we won't know when he'll hire someone to take another potshot at me."

Tracker had to hand it to her—she really knew what buttons to push.

"And I could wear a disguise. Jerry and I are about the same size—and you know how good I am at pretending to be someone else."

"I know that's what got you kidnapped last year."

"But you'll be with me tomorrow." She met his gaze squarely. "And there's another reason why you have to take me with you," she said. "We agreed when we started this that we were going to be equal partners. That's part of the deal we made—unless you're going to go back on your word."

"No." He'd never gone back on his word. He just had to make sure that he kept his word to Lucas, too. "Okay. I'll take you to the shop tomorrow morning."

She smiled at him. "Good. Now how about taking me with you to bed? Are you game for that?"

14

As Tracker eased the car onto the first road with a route number, Sophie drew in a breath of stale, air-conditioned air and tried to subtly wiggle into a more comfortable position. Jerry's jeans were cut to fit a skinny man, and they interfered with her breathing when she sat down. But, all in all, she was pleased with her disguise—especially the mustache. Tracker had supplied the materials and Jerry had supervised the application. A baseball cap hid her hair, and with the addition of mirrored sunglasses, she'd barely recognized herself in the mirror.

Sneaking a quick look at Tracker, she noted that he'd slipped into protective mode again. She didn't want to distract him. The fact that he'd put the top up on the convertible and tucked a nasty-looking rifle behind the seat had acted as a reality check—they weren't playing a game. The purpose of the disguise she was wearing was to protect her life.

"Damn," Tracker muttered.

The brakes squealed and she glanced up to see that a tree had fallen across the road. She had just time enough to brace herself before the car fishtailed and slid beneath one of the larger branches on the shoulder.

She'd barely righted herself in the seat when she heard a sharp ping and felt the car shake. Someone was shooting at them.

Tracker's hand clamped on her arm. "Do what I say. No questions."

She nodded.

He grabbed the rifle. "We're going out your door and down the hill on that side. Move."

She crawled out among branches and leaves. Tracker was right behind her, pushing her through them, and then they were half running, half falling down the sharp incline.

EVEN AFTER THEY REACHED the shelter of the woods, Tracker didn't let up his pace. He wanted to get as far into the forest as he could before he doubled back. The fact that Sophie was able to keep up with him was a surprise and a blessing. They'd been lucky so far. Very. He'd heard the sounds of bullets hitting stones twice during their mad scramble down the hill. Thank heaven there'd been one to run down and that the tree's branches had provided cover as they'd left the car.

He wasn't going to think of what might have happened if he hadn't put the top up on the convertible.

"There." He urged Sophie toward an outcrop of rock and fallen trees. He needed a place to stash her so that he could find the shooter. Once they were behind it, crouching low, he signaled her to be quiet. He listened. One minute stretched into two and then three. Gradually, he could hear other sounds above their labored breathing—wind rustling the leaves; a bird singing its heart out on a nearby branch. Another minute went by, and the branches overhead dipped and swung upward as a squirrel leaped to a new tree.

And then he heard what he'd been waiting for: the snap of a twig. Placing his hands on either side of Sophie's face, he drew her close so that he could mouth the words in her ear. "Stay put. Promise me that no matter what happens, you'll stay here."

"I promise."

Drawing back, he gave her a smile, then pulled a revolver from his pocket and handed it to her. She took it, then grabbed his T-shirt in one fist and drew him close for a quick, hard kiss. "Come back."

Another twig snapped. This one was loud enough that he could calculate the direction. Tucking the butt of the rifle under his arm, he rose and ran in a wide arc that would take him back in the direction of the road.

He didn't try to muffle his footsteps. He wanted the shooter to know where he was, wanted to lead him as far away from Sophie as he could. With all the noise he was making, there would be no way to tell that only Tracker was on the run.

In spite of the obstacles—roots, fallen trees and branches—Tracker settled into as steady a rhythm as he could, breathing in and out and letting his mind empty. Twigs snapped beneath his feet, birds shot out from the trees overhead. Any fool should be able to track him. He counted minutes off in his mind. He couldn't afford to think of Sophie now or worry about whether she'd stay put. He had to trust her and focus on the prey he would lure into his trap.

Four minutes into his run, he spotted the kind of tree he was looking for, headed toward it and grabbed for the lowest limb. Swinging himself up into the branches, he began his wait.

SOPHIE SAT CROUCHED where Tracker had left her, listening and praying. He'd told her to stay put, but she didn't think she could have moved if she'd wanted to. The cold knot of fear in her stomach numbed her. For a while she could track his progress over the carpet of dried leaves and twigs, and for that length of time, she'd known he was alive. Now all she could hear was the wind and the birds.

He'd been gone too long. The words began to run through her brain, over and over. A quick glance at her watch told her that only five minutes had ticked away since he'd left, but even now, whoever had shot at them could have found him....

More than anything, she wanted to get up and race after him. But she'd given him her word. And whoever had taken a shot at them was playing a deadly game. If she went after Tracker, she might distract him and he might be killed. Just the thought had panic sprinting through her.

Think of something else. Closing her eyes, she pictured the names on the place cards that they'd lined up on the table in Tracker's library the night before. One of those people was behind this. If she just studied their faces, she might remember what had been there tickling the edges of her mind last night.

One by one she conjured up an image of them. Studious and serious Noah with his dark-framed glasses;

the effusive Chris Chandler waving his hands, the diamond on his pinky catching the light. Millie Langford-Hughes, a fashion plate in one of her wide-brimmed hats; and Sir Winston, a twinkle in his eyes, his hands reaching to take Sophie's.

Stop. She could feel it again—that sensation of something familiar. An image, just out of her reach.

Three shots broke the stillness. Her heart leaped to her throat even as the birds flew up overhead. Tracker. As wave after wave of terror washed over her, Sophie gripped the gun he'd given her. He'd worn it close to his body, and the metal had been warm when he'd given it to her. The gun was cold now. So cold.

Was he lying on the floor of the forest, bleeding even now? No. She wouldn't let herself think that. He'd said he'd be back, and he would. She held on to the thought and willed it to be true.

Concentrating hard on that, she listened. One minute stretched into two. A squirrel raced headlong across dead leaves and up the trunk of a nearby tree. Overhead, a bird began to sing its heart out again.

Too long. Too long. The words were becoming a chant in her mind. She shouldn't have let him go. She should have made him stay with her, safe behind the rocks. She should have told him she loved him.

A twig snapped. The sound had her gripping the gun and listening hard. She bit down hard on her lip to keep from calling out Tracker's name. If it wasn't him… Letting the silence stretch, she slipped her finger over the trigger, and then, clasping the gun with both hands, she raised her arms and waited.

Another twig snapped. "Sophie? It's me."

At the sound of his voice, she let out the breath she was holding and scrambled to her feet with a sob. He stood on the other side of the outcrop of rocks. The moment she saw him, she raced around them and launched herself into his arms. "Are you all right?"

"I'm fine," he said, wrapping his arms around her. "You waited for me."

"You should trust me more. I thought…" The moment she said the words, the image that she'd been struggling against filled her mind. Tracker's body on the forest floor, lifeless, bleeding. "I heard the shots and…" As she began to tremble, she tightened her grip on him and fought against a wave of nausea.

"You should trust me more, too, Princess. There were two of them and they won't bother us anymore."

Swallowing, Sophie concentrated on the hard strength of Tracker's body pressed against hers, the steady beat of his heart. He was warm; he was real. In a minute, she'd believe it and be able to pull away. In just a minute.

TRACKER WASN'T SURE how long they stood there beneath the trees. She was alive; she was safe. The tremors moving through her were proof of that, and in just another moment, he was going to believe that they were both fine.

The two men had been professionals and, like the one currently in the hospital, they'd had top-of-the-line weapons. If the fallen tree hadn't provided cover or if the shooters hadn't chosen a place on the road where the woods had been so close…

Tracker tightened his hold on Sophie as he shoved

the thought out of his mind. It was then that he realized she was crying. A wave of weakness washed over
him, and for a moment he was afraid that his knees
were going to buckle. She wasn't making any noise,
and he doubted that she was even aware of it. But her
tears had begun to soak his T-shirt, and he felt as
helpless as he had over a year ago when she'd cried
in Lucas's office.

"Shh," he murmured as he brushed his fingers
along her cheek. "We're both fine."

"I thought I'd lost you."

"Yeah," he said roughly. Then he slipped his hand
beneath her chin and tilted her face up. Slowly, he
brushed his lips over the tears that were still wetting
her cheeks, and then lowered his mouth to hers. Her
lips were soft, and the moment they began to heat
beneath his, he felt his body begin to relax. Very gradually, he let go of the fear. She was safe, and he was
going to keep her that way.

Drawing back, he said, "C'mon."

"You're right. If we hurry, we can still make it to
the shop before I have to open up."

He stopped short and turned to stare at her. "You're
not going there. I'm taking you back to my place."

"We settled that."

"I'm unsettling it." Whirling away, he began to
pace. "I'm supposed to protect you, and I can't. I'm
not thinking objectively. If I were, I would have figured out that they could trace us to my place. They
must have tracked us through one of our cell phones.
I should have been—"

"You stop that right now! Objectively speaking, I'd

say you were doing one hell of a job protecting me so far. One hit man is in the hospital and two others are dead.''

"That's just it. There'll be more. This guy—this Puppet Master, whoever the hell he is—will just hire more hit men. I want you somewhere safe."

Sophie moved toward him then and took his hands in hers. "That's why we're going to the shop."

"Sophie—"

She squeezed his hands. "Let me finish. They knew which road you were going to take this morning. That means that they must know where your place is. How long do you think I'll be safe there? And how objective will you be at the shop if you have to keep worrying about that?''

She was making sense. She always did, and he wanted to shake her for it. "I'll take you somewhere else."

"And how long will I have to stay there? He sent two people this time. Doesn't that prove to you that he doesn't want me at the shop this morning? Think about it. He's going to be there to make sure that he gets the coin this time, and he's afraid I'll recognize him. It's the only thing that makes sense. And if I'm not there, he might slip away. I'll never be safe."

She was right. For the first time since she'd started to cry in his arms, Tracker forced himself to start thinking logically. It was the only way he was going to be able to protect her.

"Instead of arguing, we should be checking my disguise. Is my mustache still on straight?"

"Yeah," he said. And he'd have to trust that the

disguise would work, just as he'd have to trust Sophie to play her part perfectly.

"All right," he said as he tightened his grip on her hand and began to draw her with him out of the woods. "You'll come to the shop with me, but this is the way it's going to be."

SOPHIE DIDN'T LIKE Tracker's plan. She was playing the role of a customer in her own shop, with Natalie Gibbs at her side. Sophie hadn't even recognized the detective at first. All she could think of when the tall, blond man had strolled up to them on the street was that he'd looked a little familiar. It was only when Natalie had grinned at her and said, "Great disguise," that Sophie had finally figured out who she was.

Getting past Noah had been a little tricky, but the customers browsing for bargains on the outside tables were demanding a lot of his attention. Now she and Natalie were just two guys, browsing though knick-knacks and antiques.

And absolutely nothing was happening. Tracker was at the door of the shop, supposedly helping Noah out. He would run in and man the cash register when needed, but he was really screening anyone who wandered in to browse anywhere near the ceramic horse. Members of Wainwright's security force were also taking turns wandering in and out.

The clang of bells on the front door had Sophie glancing toward it, hoping for a break in her boredom, but it was just Noah.

As he hurried into the back room, she turned toward the window and pretended an interest in the display.

A moment later, he reappeared with two half gallons of lemonade. Serving cold drinks had been Noah's idea. Sophie couldn't help but note that most of the people drawn to the free lemonade in the ninety-degree heat were lingering long enough to purchase something. It wasn't the first time she realized how lucky she was to have Noah. If it turned out that he was involved in the smuggling…

Forcing the thought out of her mind, Sophie glanced at the ceramic horse sitting on a marble-topped bureau near the window. Tracker had insisted that it be set there. The two video cameras aimed at it would record anyone who seemed even remotely interested in it.

The bells on the door clanged again, and this time Meryl hurried in.

Sophie continued to feign a fascination with the items in the window. What was Meryl doing in her shop? The question had no sooner formed in her mind than she spotted Chris Chandler talking to Noah and fluttering his hands. Beyond him, she caught a glimpse of Millie Langford-Hughes and her husband, Sir Winston, making their way toward the shop. The suspects were gathering.

Millie made a beeline for Chris Chandler, but Sir Winston paused to pour himself a cup of lemonade. He was wearing a large white Panama hat to shade his face from the sun, and Sophie again felt that flicker of memory stir at the edge of her mind. What was it? What couldn't she remember? It wasn't until he leaned down and handed a glass of lemonade to the little boy tugging at his jacket that something finally clicked. *A stranger who looked familiar.*

Later, she would wonder what exactly triggered the memory—the fact that he was wearing a hat or that she'd glanced at his hands on the cup of lemonade. All she knew at the time was that she'd seen those hands before, in that shop in England where she'd met John Landry. Only the hands had belonged to a woman who'd been wearing a wide-brimmed hat, a portly woman who had rescued a ceramic vase when a child had almost dropped it.

Tracker. She had to tell him, but when she glanced toward where he'd been standing, he wasn't there.

"Problem?" Natalie asked in a very soft voice.

Out of the corner of her eye, Sophie could see Meryl examining a chess set.

"You have to get Tracker," she said as she pretended to examine the jade figurine Natalie was holding. "I can't explain, but I'm almost sure that Sir Winston is our man."

The moment Natalie moved toward the door of the shop, Sophie scanned the crowd of people milling past on the street. In a moment, they swallowed Natalie up, too, and there was still no sign of Tracker. Sophie was about to go back to the counter when she saw something else reflected in the glass: Meryl was placing a ceramic horse next to the one on the bureau. Whirling, Sophie watched her take the original horse and slip it into her bag.

"WHAT DO YOU LIKE on your hot dog, Mr. McBride?" Ramsey asked.

"I'll skip it. I don't want to stay away too long,"

Tracker said. When Ramsey had signaled to him, he'd crossed the street to join the detective.

"Relax," Ramsey said as he shot a stream of mustard on his hot dog, then added relish and onions. "My best detective is in there."

"Yeah. But a couple of our prime suspects are outside. Noah could invite them in at any time and our party could begin."

"Here," Ramsey said, handing him a bottle of ice water. "Our shooter gave me a name this morning."

"Who?" Tracker asked.

"He claims he was hired by Meryl Beacham."

"Damn it," Tracker said as he started back across the street. "She's in there with Sophie right now."

The moment Natalie Gibbs strode out of the shop, they stopped short and waited for her to join them.

"Sophie wants you," Natalie said to Tracker. "She thinks Sir Winston is our man."

Ramsey pulled out his walkie-talkie. "My men will handle Hughes."

"What's up?" Natalie asked.

"The shooter says Meryl Beacham hired him," Tracker said. "You go back in through the front. Ramsey and I will circle around through the alley. Don't tip your hand unless you have to."

SOPHIE STARED AT THE GUN that Meryl had drawn out of her purse.

"Nice disguise, Sophie," Meryl said. "I particularly like the mustache. And since I wasn't expecting you, I might even have been fooled. But when you're about to steal something priceless, you learn to keep a sharp eye out for anyone who might be working undercover.''

"Why, Meryl? Why are you involved in this?"

"Money, power," Meryl said. Then a cold smile played about her lips. "And the thrill of playing the game and outwitting everyone."

Stall. Tracker will be here. It helped not to look at the gun, so Sophie kept her eyes on the other woman's face. "You won't get away with stealing it, you know. There's a video camera on you even now."

Meryl smiled at her. "Where I'm taking this, the pictures won't matter. We'll never be caught. Now let's go. You and I are going out the back door."

Sophie held her ground. "There are security people everywhere. You won't get far."

Meryl laughed softly. "Oh, I think I'll get far enough with you as my hostage. It would have been so much simpler if you'd been killed yesterday or even today, but you seem to have nine lives." Her smile faded. "And you've caused me to lose face with my partner. For that reason alone, it would give me very great pleasure to shoot you. Start walking into the back room."

"But you won't shoot me. I'm no good to you dead."

Meryl met her eyes steadily. "That's right. But if your handsome boyfriend comes rushing in the door to save you, I'll shoot him. Move."

Don't panic, Sophie told herself. She walked slowly. Each second she could delay would give Tracker time to do something. They made it into the back hallway without anyone coming into the shop.

It was only as she punched numbers into the security pad on the back door that Sophie realized her hands were shaking. And when she tried the door, it wouldn't open.

"Stop stalling." Meryl jabbed the gun into her back. "A bullet can cause a lot of pain without killing you."

"I'm not stalling. It's a new code." This time, she went more slowly. "Is Noah in on this with you?"

"Your assistant hasn't been very efficient. His job was simple—just make sure the piece got into the hands of the right customer."

"Why would he agree to do that?" Sophie asked.

"Greed at first, and then fear. This game has very high stakes. If you fail, you die. And I don't intend to die. Open the door, Sophie."

Gripping the handle, Sophie opened the door and scanned the courtyard. It was empty.

Meryl took her arm and pressed the gun against her spine. "We're going into the alley. I left my car there. Don't try anything or I will shoot you in the back, and you'll spend the rest of your life in a wheelchair. Do you understand?"

Sophie nodded. She didn't trust herself to speak. Where was Tracker?

"And if your boyfriend shows up, warn him to stay away. Understood?"

Sophie nodded again.

The gun jabbed into her back. "Answer me, Sophie."

"Yes," she managed to reply. "I understand."

And then they were walking slowly across the flagstones. Just as they stepped out into the alleyway, Tracker spoke. "Drop the gun, Meryl."

Sophie had time to register where he was standing, just to Meryl's right. And then Meryl was swinging the gun toward him. She saw Tracker make his move and, in the same instant, Sophie launched herself at Meryl's gun arm.

As her fingers closed around the woman's wrist, she saw the flash of fire, heard the deafening explosion and then they were both tumbling to the ground. Sophie felt her head strike something hard, and saw a bright explosion of fireworks. Through them, she saw Tracker subdue Meryl and Ramsey slip handcuffs on her wrists.

There was something important that she had to tell Tracker, but when she tried to sit up, she couldn't seem to lift her head. It hurt. Then Tracker was beside her and he was running his hands over her, expertly, thoroughly, the way he always did in her dream. Relaxing, she closed her eyes and started to drift.

"You're bleeding!"

The shouted words dragged her back to consciousness. Opening her eyes, she tried to focus, but now there were two Trackers bending over her. "You're not supposed to yell. You're supposed to say, 'You're safe, Princess.'"

"Damn it, Sophie! Did she shoot you? Where?"

"Ouch! Don't touch my head. I think it's broken. But you can touch me everywhere else."

"Get an ambulance!"

He wasn't supposed to yell. That wasn't part of her

dream. "Tracker." She couldn't see him quite as well now. Everything was turning gray.

"Shh." He took her hand. "Don't talk."

"Winston Hughes. I think he's the Puppet Master."

Then she closed her eyes and slipped into the dream that was waiting for her.

SOPHIE SAT UP in the hospital bed and threw her legs over the side. Her headache had settled into a dull throb just about where the stitches were, and she wasn't seeing double anymore. There was only one Mac sitting in the chair near her bed, her concerned gaze on Sophie. And there was only one Chess sitting on her lap. Lucas had smuggled him in.

"I'm getting dressed."

"The doctors want you to stay another night," Mac said firmly. "They don't like to fool around with concussions."

"I'm fine."

Chess let out a disgusted snort.

Sophie glared at him. "Don't you start. I'm fine, and I have to get out of here because I have to track someone down." She hadn't seen Tracker for over twenty-four hours, and a cold fear had begun to build in her.

"Sophie, if you get out of bed, I'm going to have to get up and out of this chair." Mac paused to run a hand gently over her belly. "And the baby just fell asleep."

Sophie tried her best to scowl at her friend. "That's blackmail."

"Whatever works. I promised Lucas and Tracker that I would keep you here until they arrived."

Sophie's eyes narrowed. "When will they get here?"

"Whenever they finish up at the police station. Lucas called while the doctor was with you and filled me in on the latest. Millie Langford-Hughes has been fully cleared. The only thing she seems to be guilty of is marrying cads. Meryl's attorney advised her to take the deal they were offering, and she's singing her heart out. They'll be able to nail Sir Winston Hughes. He was trying to say that the two coins they found in his wall safe were ones he purchased in good faith."

"And Noah?" Sophie asked.

"He was told that he would receive the backing to open his own shop if he would just help out. According to Meryl, that was the 'carrot.' When Jayne Childress was killed, he caught on that the little game they were playing was a deadly one. He continued to go along with them because he was afraid for his life."

"I'm going to hire him an attorney," Sophie said. "In his place, I might have done the same thing. He couldn't have known what he was getting into at first."

"Tracker predicted that you would do that," Mac said.

"Really." The man seemed to have time to talk to everyone but her.

"Really," a male voice echoed.

She turned and felt her heart lurch when she saw him standing in the doorway with Lucas. Relief warred with an almost overwhelming desire to run right into his arms. But she had a game plan.

"I think I'm beginning to understand the way your mind works, Princess."

She lifted her chin. "We have to talk."

Mac rose from her chair. "C'mon, Lucas. Let's take a walk down to the nursery. I'd offer to take Chess, but I don't think the nurses would approve."

TRACKER DIDN'T THINK he'd ever seen a room cleared quite so efficiently. "Nice going, Princess."

The temper in her voice and the stiffness in her spine assured him, more than anything her doctors had said, that Sophie was going to be all right. Even wearing a faded hospital gown and a bandage on her head, she looked every inch the Princess. The fear that had been rolling around inside of him since he'd realized that she was bleeding in that alley began to fade.

She was safe, and so was he. And he had a plan. Since he figured Sophie might have one of her own, he locked the door. Then he held out the daisies he'd been hiding behind his back. "These are for you."

She stared at them. "You brought me flowers."

"Yes." Since she didn't seem inclined to take them, he laid them in her lap.

"Why? No." She raised a hand to stop him before he could reply. "You brought them because you're a kind, sweet man. And they're beautiful." She lifted them and held them to her face for a moment.

So far so good, he thought. He was just about to reach for the box in his pocket when he saw the first tear roll down her cheek. "Sophie?"

She tossed the flowers at him, then swiped impatiently at her cheeks. "I know exactly what you're doing. You're giving them to me to soften the blow when you tell me that you don't want to see me again. You'll probably bring up some baloney about how we don't have anything in common. We come from different worlds. And then you'll slink off into your shadows again. Well, I'm not having it."

"You're not?" He'd been dead wrong. He still didn't have a clue about the way her mind worked.

"No." She swiped at her cheeks again. "I don't want to have an affair with you anymore."

The pain hit him like a sucker punch in the gut.

"No-strings affairs aren't much better than one-night stands. Either one of us could decide to pack up and go."

She met his eyes, and he saw all of the fears that he had been feeling for the past twenty-four hours reflected in them. She was every bit as afraid of losing him as he was of losing her. How could he have thought they were so different when they were so much alike?

"I want to marry you," she stated.

For the second time in as many minutes, he felt as though he'd been punched low and hard. "Sophie." He moved toward her then, but she raised a hand.

"You can't talk me out of it. It's marriage or nothing."

Tracker opened his mouth and shut it. So much for the proposal he'd planned. There was just no predicting his Sophie. Slowly, he smiled. "We're getting married."

She frowned. "I'm not joking. We'll just settle it the way we started—with a coin toss." After slipping off the bed, she walked to the cupboard and fished a coin out of her jeans. "Heads, we get married. Tails, you can go off with your horses and Jerry and we never see each other again."

"Okay."

She whirled to look at him then. "You're willing to settle our future on the toss of a coin?"

"I'm game for it if you are."

Her eyes narrowed and heated. "Great! Oh, that's just fine and dandy. You're ready to let our whole future be decided by some silly game!"

"I thought you wanted me to learn to go with the flow."

He saw the flash of fire in her eyes, and before she could work up enough steam to punch him, he went to her, took her in his arms and settled her back on the bed. Then he sat down beside her and took her hands. "Sophie, I'm game for it because you're using a two-headed coin."

She stared at him then. "How did you...?"

"I gave that coin to Mac as a wedding gift. I knew that she was collecting stuff for her research. I thought she'd get a kick out of it."

"You've known all along?"

"No. I figured it out about the second or third time you tossed it. It always came up heads."

She thought for a minute. "I still want to get married."

"Why don't we try it a more traditional way?" He dropped to his knees and then drew out the box from his pocket and opened it. "I love you, Sophie Wainwright, and I want you to marry me."

Sophie stared down at the ring. The diamond in the center was surrounded by stones in every color of the rainbow. She felt a tear escape.

"It's not a traditional ring. You can exchange it if you want, but it reminded me of you."

"I love it." The moment he slipped it on her finger, she felt another tear escape. Others filled her throat as she met his eyes. "I love you, T.J. McBride, and I was so afraid of losing you."

"Me, too, Princess." He gathered her close and rested his cheek on her hair. "We're a lot alike."

Chess gave a satisfied sigh from his ringside seat on the chair.

Sophie drew back from Tracker then. "If we're so much alike, then you must know what I'm thinking."

He narrowed his eyes.

"Relax. I'm just thinking that you gave me two presents and I haven't given you anything." After reaching for her purse, she pulled out the coupon and handed it to him.

He grinned at her. He'd been prepared for this surprise, at least—he'd locked the door. "Here?"

"Now."

"Your wish is my command, Princess."

Her teeth were busy at his ear as he pressed her back against the bed. Seconds later, he'd freed himself and tested her. She was so wet, so ready, so his.

She nipped at his ear and whispered, "I've got the black ribbon in there, too…if you're game."

"Not until you get out of the hospital," he said as

he eased himself into her and felt the completion he always experienced when they were joined. "Then, as long as I'm with you, I'm game for anything."

"Me, too, T.J. Me, too."

Joined as one, they began to move.

Epilogue

"I don't want to leave you."

Tracker bit back a smile as he unpacked the picnic basket Jerry had prepared. The Princess was in rare form, pacing back and forth beneath the willow tree. Not even a wild chase across the fields on Persephone had settled her nerves. Well, he could relate to that. His own stomach was jittery, too. Getting married wasn't something that a man did every day, and he wanted to do it right.

"Who came up with the ridiculous tradition that a bride can't see her groom on their wedding day? I told Mac I didn't want to have any part of it."

And that's when Tracker had gotten the emergency phone call from Mac. He poured wine into two glasses and reviewed his game plan. After four months of being together, he was still trying to come up with a method for handling Sophie. Something told him it was going to take a lifetime—a lifetime of colorful passion and challenge and love. He could deal with that.

"I don't see why I have to spend the night before our wedding on the Wainwright estate and leave you here alone," she complained.

Several responses occurred to Tracker, and each one

held the potential for disaster. Dr. MacKenzie Lloyd Wainwright was a woman on a mission. It amazed him that a research scientist who was eight months pregnant could have the time or the energy to plan a wedding. But Mac had thrown herself into the job with the energy and determination of a five-star general. She was determined to give Sophie a perfect day.

On that point, their goals meshed. He could only hope that his current strategy would work.

Sophie stopped pacing and tapped her foot. "You're not saying anything. Do you agree with Mac? Do you want to spend the night away from me?"

Time to face the firing squad. "Yes, to your first question, and I'm going to pass on the second."

"Pass?" She narrowed her eyes. "You're doing that on purpose so that you can collect a penalty."

He grinned at her and held out a hand. "You can see right through me, Princess."

She moved toward him slowly. "And I suppose you think you can distract me and pacify me with sex."

"That's my game plan."

The moment she lowered herself to the blanket beside him, he took her hands and said, "But first I have a question of my own, and I want you to answer it."

SOPHIE COULD TELL by the sudden change in his eyes that he was serious. "Okay."

"Are you reluctant to follow the tradition because you're still afraid that I might walk away from you?"

In his eyes, she saw, as she often did, the perfect mirror of her own doubts and fears. How could she forget that they were so much alike? She willed her own nerves to settle, and tightened her grip on his hands. "No. I'm not afraid of that anymore."

"Good. Then I agree with Mac that we ought to spend the night before our wedding apart. I think I'm turning into a traditional kind of guy."

The thought of that made Sophie want to laugh and cry at the same time. "Not too traditional, I hope."

He grinned at her. "Just traditional enough to want to give my bride a wedding gift—and untraditional enough to want you to open it right now."

When he pulled the small box out of his pocket, she stared at it. "This isn't the penalty, is it?"

"Trust me, Princess."

She did, and after opening the box, she found two halves of a gold coin strung on a narrow black velvet ribbon. "T.J., it's beautiful."

"It's us," he said as he lifted it and tied the ribbon at the back of her neck. "Tonight, when we're apart, I want you to wear this and remember that we're two halves of the same coin."

Even as her eyes began to fill, she drew him close, and when their mouths met, she poured herself into the kiss until she felt that sense of oneness that he was talking about.

Before she lost herself in him completely, Tracker drew back a little. "And the black ribbon is supposed to remind you of something else, too."

She smiled at him, wondering how it was that he could make her want to cry one minute and laugh the next. Then she pushed him onto his back and straddled him. "I haven't forgotten. One of these days, I'll get the thing with the ribbon right. I just need a little more practice.''

He grinned up at her. ''I can offer you a lifetime of practice, Princess.''

''Deal.'' Leaning down, she covered his mouth with hers.

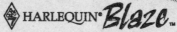

Bestselling author Tori Carrington
delves into the very *private*
lives of two *public* defenders, in:

LEGAL BRIEFS

Don't miss:

#65 FIRE AND ICE
December 2002
&
#73 GOING TOO FAR
February 2003

Come feel the heat!

**Available wherever
Harlequin books are sold.**

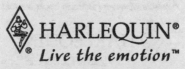

HARLEQUIN® *Blaze*™

From:	**Erin Thatcher**
To:	**Samantha Tyler;**
	Tess Norton
Subject:	**Men To Do**

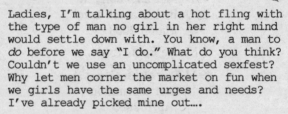

Ladies, I'm talking about a hot fling with
the type of man no girl in her right mind
would settle down with. You know, a man to
do before we say "I do." What do you think?
Couldn't we use an uncomplicated sexfest?
Why let men corner the market on fun when
we girls have the same urges and needs?
I've already picked mine out....

**Don't miss the steamy new Men To Do miniseries
from bestselling Blaze authors!**

THE SWEETEST TABOO by Alison Kent
December 2002

A DASH OF TEMPTATION by Jo Leigh
January 2003

A TASTE OF FANTASY by Isabel Sharpe
February 2003

Available wherever Harlequin books are sold.

HARLEQUIN®
Makes any time special ®

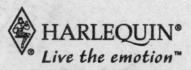